The Promise

Robert Stevenson, second from the left, and John Cameron, centre.
(Courtesy of BC Archives, G-03767)

The Promise

LOVE, LOYALTY AND THE LURE OF GOLD

~

THE STORY OF "CARIBOO" CAMERON

Bill Gallaher

TouchWood Editions are an imprint of Horsdal & Schubart Publishers Ltd., Victoria, BC, Canada.

Cover and book design by Public Art & Design, Victoria, BC.
Cover images courtesy of BC Archives, G-03767, D-07952, image manipulation by Public Art & Design, Victoria, BC.
This book is set in Garamond.

We acknowledge the support of The Canada Council for the Arts for our publishing program. We also wish to acknowledge the financial support of the Government of Canada through the Book Publishing Industry Development Program (BPDIP) for our publishing activities. We also acknowledge the financial support of the Province of British Columbia through the British Columbia Arts Council.

Printed and bound in Canada by Friesens, Altona, Manitoba.

National Library of Canada Cataloguing in Publication Data

Gallaher, Bill.
  The promise

  Includes bibliographical references.
  ISBN 0-920663-75-3

  1. Cameron, John Angus, 1820-1888--Fiction.   I. Title.
PS8563.A424P76 2001   C813'.6   C2001-910321-2
PR9199.4.G256P76 2001

Printed and bound in Canada

For Jaye, always

Contents

Acknowledgments

A book is more than an idea expressed with written words. These are merely the author's contributions. That I enjoyed the time to write it is due to my wife, Jaye Gallagher; that it is coherent is due to the editorial skills of Marlyn Horsdal; and that it was deemed fit for a life of its own on the printed page is due to Marlyn and Pat Touchie. My sincere thanks to all of these good people.

Others should be thanked as well: Richard Thomas Wright for an evening's conversation during a busy haying season; Cheryl Isaac for the information on Caroline Stevenson; and most particularly Philip Teece, for reading the original manuscript and offering encouragement and sound advice.

Introduction

When the *Titanic* went down in 1912, among the many souls taken with it were Isador and Ida Straus, an elderly couple who married as youngsters. After helping others to the lifeboats, Isador tried to force Ida into one without him. She climbed in, but immediately climbed back out. Grabbing his arm, she said, "We've been together a great many years. Where you go, I will go."

They were reported to have sat side by side in deck chairs as the ship sank. Isador's body was recovered, Ida's never was.

Such stories of utter loyalty and friendship fascinate me. (Let me be clear here, and state my belief that workable marriages usually happen because the husband and wife have become friends.) It causes me to wonder how far I would be willing to go in my relationships with others, what sacrifices I would be willing to make; would I ever draw the line and say, "Enough is enough. I will go this far and no further"? In other words, had I been in Ida's shoes, would I have stayed in the lifeboat?

Luckily, most of us manage to get through life without having our relationships so severely tested, but every now and then, fate or chance or God or whatever one chooses to name it, intervenes in the lives of some people and forces difficult choices upon them. Usually not as extreme as in the Strauses' case, but life-affecting nonetheless. And how they respond invariably provides the true measure of their loyalty and of what it means to be a friend.

Such was the case with Robert Stevenson and his friends, John and Sophia Cameron. When I first read their incredible story, it drew me in completely, not so much because of the harrowing journey the two men made, but because of their reasons for making it. The three came together by chance during the spring of 1862, in Victoria, British Columbia, harbouring dreams of gold. History has shown that two of them found it, in great quantities. It has also shown that the path to discovery was marred by tragedies, culminating in Sophia's death. But such was the depth of the two men's loyalty to her that in the end, gold was not all that shone in their lives.

On the part of one there was lustre in a fulfilled promise to a dying wife, and on the part of the other, in a selfless offer to help fulfil that promise. Without any of these words being spoken, this is what was asked of each of them: "Would you cross a mountain range, on foot, in the dead of winter, through sub-zero temperatures and snow deeper than a man is tall, then slip and slide up and down ice-clad roads edged with deadly, precipitous drop-offs, while pulling and pushing a human cargo that in every likelihood is oblivious to your titanic struggle, yet is all the more precious for it? Would you do this day after day, week after week, until the task was done?"

And each man replied with his actions: "I will do it. I will take this step, and another, and another, if necessary, and I will see it through to the end, because it is my duty as a friend."

Yet a fascination with loyalty in friendships is not the only parent of this book. The other is a song.

As a singer and songwriter of historical ballads, I am always looking for new material, interesting vignettes of history that help illuminate Canada as a country. When I stumbled across the Cameron-Stevenson story, it seemed to me that it was more than just another gold rush tale and more than an eloquent statement of great loyalty among friends. It was also about Canada and Canadians, something that defined us as a people, and it begged to be made into a song.

My first instinct was to write a ballad but to do the story justice, a ballad would probably end up being far too long, which would diminish both its power and its appeal for audiences. It needed to be broken up. So I wrote a short song about a specific scene and performed it in conjunction with a brief narration — an outline, really — of the story.

But it is woefully lacking in details, and I've always felt a need to tell it at greater length. A book seemed to be the logical solution. Further research turned up other material, but certainly the best was the memoir written by Stevenson himself, which provides the skeleton for this book. The flesh of it is my doing.

So here, in a way, is the ballad that I never wrote, one without music or rhyme, but a ballad nevertheless.

Bill Gallaher, Victoria, BC

Chapter One

I FIRST MET the Camerons by chance in the early spring of 1862. Had I been able to foresee the extraordinary events our meeting would lead to, that we would forge a tale that would survive long after their departure from this earth, and will likely do so long after mine, I would have thought it the wildest of dreams.

We all three were raised by Loyalist families in Glengarry County in Canada West, which these days is known as Ontario. The county lies along the St. Lawrence River, just east of the township of Cornwall, the county seat. It was mostly rural then, and still is, dotted here and there with farms and small communities; an eye-pleasing landscape continually refreshed by the seasons. We had grown up within just a few miles of each other but had never met. Ironically, that would have to wait for another time and another place — one nearly 3,000 miles away.

I speak of Victoria, that strangest of towns in what was then the colony of Vancouver Island. By strange, I mean that beyond the collection of wooden and brick buildings that stood on the slope above the harbour, which were certainly pleasing enough to the eye, it was virtually a city of tents and shanties. Low peaks of canvas tilted every which way alongside slapdash plank shelters, all lodgings for miners waiting for winter to pass and the trails to Cariboo to be free of snow.

I was there for the very same reason but could afford to take a room at the Royal Hotel near the corner of Wharf and Johnson streets. It was one of the few brick buildings in town and boasted board and lodging at only eight dollars a week. My room was small but adequate and consisted of a wardrobe, a washstand with a porcelain basin and ewer, a mirror, a wooden armchair with an upholstered seat already stained, a four-poster bed with a mattress more comfortable than anything I'd slept on for some time and a chamberpot stowed discreetly beneath it. A single framed lithograph hung from an interior wall thin enough to spit through. A window overlooked Wharf Street and I welcomed the noise of creaking wagons, chuffing horses, and chattering people, even the clanging bells and throaty whistles of ships in the harbour, for I was invigorated to have civilization so near at hand.

A panoramic view of Victoria in 1858, taken from the harbour, looking up View Street with some of Wharf Street showing on the left. The stone building second from the right is the Police Barracks on Langley Street, which also served as the town jail and law court. The yard to the left of the jail, now called Bastion Square, is where public hangings took place, and the false-fronted building at the centre is the Boomerang Saloon.
(COURTESY OF BC ARCHIVES G-04780)

As a wintering spot in these northern climes, Victoria was as good a place as any in which to spend time, and better than most, I expect. It had changed in the two-and-a-half years since my first visit, transformed by gold from the Fraser River. Back then, it wasn't much more than a Hudson's Bay Company fort with a few houses and shops built around it. Now the fort had all but disappeared, replaced by a town of fair size. Where there were once a few hundred year-round inhabitants, there were now several thousand, not including transients like me and those living in that sea of tents, who must have also numbered in the thousands. On any given weekday, the town was busy with the hustle and bustle of commerce and the general transactions of humanity. And the topic of most conversations was gold.

I had at least four months to spend before the mining season reopened and I had every intention of putting them to good use. Since my wilderness sojourns had not allowed much time for the luxury of reading, I spent hours perusing books at the new reading library over on Fort Street, which of all places epitomized just how much Victoria had grown and how civilized it was becoming.

I walked the city often, from end to end and from top to bottom, peering into shop windows, chatting with merchants, and watching the townspeople going about their daily business: bonneted women wrapped in shawls, frock-coated men, others roughly clad, still others in uniforms of the Royal Marines and Royal Navy, and children oblivious to all but themselves. When I wanted to step lively, I sought country roads that ultimately led to outlying farms in Saanich and Cadboro Bay. Occasionally I went to view the ships in Esquimalt's harbour, but the road there was often so clogged with pedestrian and vehicular traffic that walking it was rarely a pleasant experience.

After a good rain, it was always prudent to stick to the boardwalks and wooden crosswalks where such conveniences existed, or you risked finding yourself ankle deep in mud. Quite frankly, mud is what I remember most about Victoria that winter. Rumours abounded that it hid potholes in which small horses and carriages sometimes vanished. When conditions got so bad that the crosswalks began disappearing, a chain gang from the jail was dispatched to clean up the streets. (There was rarely a shortage of prisoners available for the task, as it was a time when a person could be sent to jail for something as simple as an unpaid debt. Indeed, a carpenter named Edward Dillon had just been jailed for that very reason. He had done some work for the local Jockey Club and was unable to pay off his materials supplier when the club, for whatever reason, defaulted on their payments to him.) Recently, the town had begun a badly needed project of macadamizing the streets, but so far, only Store Street was done and no one was holding their breath till another was completed.

The town was more than mud, of course. I remember with equal clarity its smells and sounds. Concerning the former, I speak not of pretty flower gardens and heady fragrances, not even of the wood and coal smoke that was persistently present, but of the stale reek of saloons, the urine-soaked stench of horse manure from stables, the almost sweet scent of fresh equine deposits in the street and the stink of sewage-filled gutters along the boardwalks, rotting garbage behind an assortment of eating establishments, and human waste. It was a welcome breeze that swept in off the sea, or out of the Sooke Hills, from time to time.

Loosely woven through the warp of smells was a weft of sounds. As well as the ships in the harbour, the horses and wagons and a buzz of voices, there were the thunder of boots on the wooden boardwalks, the shouts of a town crier with the latest shipping news, the ring of a blacksmith's hammer shaping metal, and the clamour of carpenters raising new buildings. Even the tranquillity of Sunday mornings was broken by church bells and their solemn summons to early devotions.

A photograph taken from just about any corner in Victoria would probably have a saloon somewhere in it. There was an abundance of them, for drinking was a common pastime for most men, especially miners when they were idle and had money. Most were grotty little places, but a few strove for respectability. The Boomerang Saloon over by the Police Barracks was such an establishment and, though my own drinking habits were modest, evenings would sometimes find me there talking at length with other miners and listening to their stories of fortunes made and lost, and fortunes sure to come. Everyone had a tale to tell and though I bore no reluctance to tell mine, I deemed it more profitable to listen. There was much to be learned from men with years of placer-mining experience, who knew how to make a gravel bar yield its riches. So I kept my ears and mind open and asked more questions than were answered for me.

One night a man named Abbot, who had struck it rich in Cariboo, found himself in such fine humour from his good fortune and grog that he hurled a handful of gold pieces against the mirror behind the bar, shattering it into countless shards. Over the utter silence that engulfed the place, he told the barkeeper to buy a new one and "keep the change." Since the "change" was an extraordinarily generous amount, every saloon owner in town was hoping for a visit from Abbot. On another night, a newly rich miner stood drinks for the house and when the bill didn't come to much, he ordered the barkeeper to fill every empty glass in the place and set them on the bar. That done, he swept them crashing to the floor with his arm.

When I was not of a mind for company, I'd buy the *British Colonist* for ten cents, find an empty corner somewhere and read about what was happening around town and the colonies. There were reports, almost daily, of the war raging between America's northern and southern states that I followed with great interest. The conflict was so young then I could not have imagined that it would go on for as long as it did, with such ferocity and appalling loss of life.

It wasn't always necessary to buy a daily paper for information. Some of the best news could be obtained at Frank Campbell's tobacco store on the corner of Yates and Government, next door to the Adelphi Saloon. The locals called it "Campbell's Corner." He'd post the latest news bulletins in his window, particularly those having anything to do with gold. People also went there to hear the latest gossip, most of which flared up and died like a match. It wasn't unusual to see a crowd standing around, the size of which always depended on the quality of the latest news or gossip. It was how idle men without much money passed the time of day.

And there was no shortage of idle men in Victoria that winter. There were throngs of them, mostly miners in limbo, impatient for spring to arrive. The majority of them were getting by, but more than a few were looking for handouts. It wasn't unusual to be approached by a down-and-out miner for a half-dollar to put a square meal or a drink in his belly, much to the annoyance of many a passerby. But I could never resist such entreaties. Had it not been for God's good grace, it might easily have been me with my hat in hand.

And so the time passed. January was freezing as the temperature fell to 17 degrees below zero and it snowed heavily. New Westminster, the capital of British Columbia, was ice-bound and the only way it could be reached was by a seven-mile trail from Mud Bay, near Point Roberts, and a five-mile trail from Burrard Inlet. Its citizens were as isolated there as they would have been in any place near the North Pole. Victoria was the only port north of San Francisco that was open, although one morning the harbour was covered with a thin skin of ice, and in Rock

The view south along Government Street. The building on the left is the Little Brown Jug Saloon, and jutting into the sky on the far right are "The Birdcages"—the name given to the earliest Legislative Buildings because of their appearance. (COURTESY OF BC ARCHIVES A-03015)

Bay, it was thick enough that some boys were actually able to skate on it. Snow lay white and thick upon the town and in the south Saanich countryside it was knee-deep. Men and boys made good sport of it by heaving snowballs into sleighs passing up and down Government Street, but its most redeeming quality was that it froze and covered the muddy streets, and served at night to brighten up the town, which was usually as dark as a coal pit.

For a while, time and the town seemed to hang in limbo, almost like a bear in hibernation, until even the newspapers were hard-pressed to come up with a newsworthy story. They were "Dull Times," the editor of the *Colonist* reported, adding, "We don't wish to advise any of our readers to commit a felony, but if somebody were to go and do something desperate to somebody else, he would confer a great favor on us, which we would repay with the publication of his name in the largest type in the office. Is the inducement sufficient?"[1]

As if in answer to the editor's prayers an incident arose on Government Street that proved newsworthy. A Negro was strolling along the boardwalk when he was hit in the back of the head by a snowball. He looked around and the only person close enough to have thrown it was a white man. The Negro launched himself at his attacker and a fight ensued with punches thrown and the two men wrestling on the ground while a crowd gathered round. No one showed the least bit of interest in halting the proceedings, since here at last was something to break up the monotony. Finally, the police arrived and separated the two men who were none the worse for wear, a cut chin on one and a bloody nose on the other notwithstanding.

This incident was by no means unusual in Victoria, which numbered many Negroes among its citizens, most of them driven north because of oppressive conditions in the United States. During the fall of 1861, a benefit concert was held at a local theatre to raise money for a new hospital. Several Negroes — mostly prominent businessmen with their wives — bought the best seats in the house for the performance, which put a few white noses out of joint. Someone provided onions to hurl at the intruders to neutralize their "Ethiopian odours."[2]

It will come as no surprise that the Negroes were angered by this offensive behaviour, but, much to their credit, they responded only by refusing to move. When one of the whites threw flour over a Negro's head, however, they'd had enough and a fight broke out. The police were called in to break it up and several participants were charged with assault. The whites involved were acquitted, while one Negro was found guilty and fined.

January turned into February as I attended a series of lectures on Modern Novelists given by the Reverend J. Hall, an animated orator who one evening spoke on the topic of "Novels of Sensation." I was thus inspired to return to the library the following day to read Wilkie Collins' *The Woman in White*, a sinister tale of mystery and intrigue, and certainly one of the most unusual books I had ever read. I also attended a lecture, sponsored by the Literary Institute and given by Alfred Waddington, on minerals and mining. I found him to be a brusquely confident man, rather caught up in himself, but knowledgeable in his chosen field, although one can take only so many diagrams of how minerals crystallize and coal is mined in France. Far more interesting than Waddington, in my estimation, were the nightly shows at the Lyceum Melodeon and the Theatre Royal. Though much of the entertainment was unabashedly commonplace, it was usually an enjoyable experience. I found a performance of Ethiopian eccentricities, ballads, and dance particularly amusing.

Since the Royal Hotel had no baths, I could usually be found on Saturday nights at the Pioneer Shaving Saloon and Bath House, an especially genial place run by an astute Negro from the Cayman Islands. His name was Wellington Moses and he was just one of several Negro businessmen who had come to Victoria to start a new life. He was doing quite well for himself too, and might have continued had he handled his personal affairs as well as he ran his business.

Moses had an eye for the ladies but blundered when he failed to keep the other eye firmly fixed on his wife. When she discovered his infidelities, her despair was such that she tried to kill herself by jumping into the harbour. When the newspapers got hold of that choice piece of news, Moses reckoned it was time to move on. Not long after I knew him he sold the baths and went north to Cariboo. It took him a while, but he eventually ended up in Barkerville where he opened a barbershop.

In 1866 Moses was returning after a visit to the coast when, at Yale, he teamed up with a white man named Charles Blessing. They travelled north together and met a third man, John Barry, who joined the pair. At Quesnellemouth, Moses had some business to attend to, so the two white men went on ahead, promising to meet him at Van Winkle, on the road into Barkerville.[3] Moses got there a couple of days later and, finding neither Barry nor Blessing, went on to Barkerville. Later he ran into Barry and asked what happened to Blessing. Barry's answers were vague enough that Moses suspected foul play. Two subsequent meetings only served to increase Moses' suspicions.

Then a customer arrived at Moses' barbershop wearing a gold nugget tie pin that he knew belonged to Blessing. The customer said he got it from a Hurdy Gurdy, a dancing girl from one of the saloons. Moses sought out the Hurdy who told him she got the pin from Barry, at which point the barber went directly to the constable at Richfield, arriving there about the same time as Blessing's body was discovered. The local constable went after Barry, who was heading south, and brought him back to Richfield. At his trial, he tried at first to shift the blame to Moses, but eventually confessed. Matthew Baillie Begbie was the presiding judge and sentenced Barry to death by hanging.[4]

Moses lived out his life in Barkerville, respected there as a businessman as much as he had been in Victoria, where he ran a clean establishment with fair rates considering the lack of competition. I would visit the Pioneer at least once a week — whether I felt in need of it or not — and soak in a deep tub brimming with steaming hot water. It also provided a perfect epilogue to the carnal pleasures proffered by some of the town's finer and more discreet ladies of the evening.

In the meantime, I had begun making preparations for my return to Cariboo. There appeared to be no end of business opportunities for a man with a clear view of the road ahead of him and some capital behind. I could also see that the most profitable of them would require a partner, yet so far, I'd not met anyone with whom I wished to embark on such a relationship. That ended on a particularly dull day at the beginning of March when I was resting in my room, impatient for the snow and ice to give way to spring so that I could be moving on.

John "Cariboo" Cameron. (COURTESY OF BC ARCHIVES A-01155)

I was surprised by a knock at the door and wondered who it might be. I had made no appointments and was therefore not expecting anyone. I opened the door to a handsome but sober-looking man, about 40, with wavy brown hair receding from his forehead, and a full beard that hung to the lapels of his jacket. There was an uncommon air of assurance about him, but what commanded my attention most was his eyes, an unusually deep brown, with a gaze that gripped as tight as his handshake, yet hid the man lurking behind them. He introduced himself as John Cameron from Glengarry County, Canada West. He had arrived just the day before from San Francisco on the sidewheeler *Brother Jonathan* with his wife and infant daughter. Upon registering at the desk, he was told by Mr. Wilcox, the hotel's owner, that another guest was also from Glengarry and he was kindly given my room number.

His arrival boosted my spirits immensely. As a tried and true Glengarrian, I was heartened to meet someone from home in a town that teemed with strangers from places of which I'd never heard. We exchanged pleasantries, after which he led me to his room at the rear of the hotel to meet his wife.

Sophia Cameron was nearly as tall as her husband. Her face was a harmony of lovely, soft features accented by long, raven-black hair that was pulled back and tied in a bun. Her skin had a slight bronze cast to it and seemed so smooth that I thought silk merchants might scour the Orient forever and not find a cloth as fine. She carried herself like someone going off to a soiree at a governor's manor rather than to a rough-and-tumble mining camp, and there was such grace and beauty in her movements that I was hopelessly drawn to her, though her mahogany eyes promised nothing more than the moment. Even so, I felt a red heat rising from beneath my collar that

Sophia Cameron. (COURTESY OF BC ARCHIVES D-07952)

flooded my face, but to my credit, I was able to refrain from babbling like an idiot.

We talked for a while, and it would have been a dull mind indeed that did not sense the Camerons' comfort with each other, and the warmth of their relationship. Both spoke of a mutual devotion that Sophia did not bother to hide, and her husband, despite his reserve, could not.

She smiled easily, but looked haggard and drawn after their long sea journey, and lines of worry marked her exquisite face. Their daughter had come down with a fever and even though they'd obtained medicine for her in San Francisco, her condition hadn't improved at all. Sophia had just put the little girl down to sleep and looked ready to enjoy some solitude and rest herself.

I suggested to Cameron that the two of us might walk up to the Boomerang for a whiskey. He asked Sophia if she minded some time on her own, to which she replied wearily, "After five days in steerage, John? I think not."

The day had turned remarkably brighter in the company of this man, and I don't think I stopped chattering as we cut through Waddington Alley and up Yates to the Boomerang. In the convivial atmosphere of the bar, thick with the smell of men, liquor, tobacco smoke and camphor, not to mention the never-ending tales of gold, Cameron and I began forging the bonds of a friendship that neither of us knew would last a lifetime. Before long he was insisting on knowing the road that had brought me to Victoria.

Chapter Two

FOR ME, THE road had begun three years earlier when my father first revealed his intention to go prospecting for gold. We were living on a farm in Glengarry County, near the village of Williamstown — about ten miles northeast of Cornwall — where I was born in 1838, only a few months after that fiery reformer Mackenzie marched on Toronto with his ill-equipped band of farmers. My parents had bought the land after emigrating from Northern Ireland in 1831 and had a brood of 12 kids to work it. We kept a small orchard, along with some cattle, sheep, pigs and geese, so we lived quite comfortably.

Perhaps because she could never get a word in edgewise, my mother was a quiet woman who doted on her children. As a consequence, she rarely experienced a moment's rest. My father was a good-humoured and wise man. It is to him that I owe much of what I have been and what I now am, for he pointed out the stars that I have used to navigate through life. If people are to trust you, he said, then you must be responsible, and the amount of responsibility that you accept becomes your measure as a man. It followed that to give a man responsibility is to show you trust him, and trust is the cement that holds all human relationships together. It is better to be deceived by a friend, he insisted, than to distrust him. He also believed that no matter how poor you are, you can always afford to be generous, even if it means giving only of your time. He himself lived by those words and was trusted implicitly by all, including me. And if you needed a helping hand, he would be the first to extend his.

I had only just left my teen years behind me when my father began talking of gold. He had heard the stories that spread through the Canadas like an infectious disease, tales of vast fortunes being made with a single swoop and swirl of water and gravel in a pan, or even more outrageous, of gold nuggets lying everywhere, just waiting for an enterprising person to bend over and pick them up. Soon, men of all ages and from all walks of life were leaving behind secure jobs and families, in most cases with more optimism and passion than the circumstances warranted. Yet, leave they did, with their sights fixed unfalteringly on the golden shores of British Columbia.

As he did with much of what he heard, my father listened to those tales with a skeptical ear. But there was an undeniable streak of optimism and passion in him too, and he said that if there was only an ounce of truth to the stories (or even better, several ounces!), then a trip to the new colony would be well worth the time and effort. Such talk made my mother anxious, especially when my father's plans included me, but in the end she gave her consent, knowing full well that the two of us would not be satisfied until we were westward bound.

I was just 21 years old, but I was big and strong as an ox and had no fear of hard work. And though it wasn't my nature to go out of my way to look for trouble, I was confident that I could handle any that came along. We knew we would be tested, as the territory we were headed for was far from being civilized and if the mosquitoes and flies didn't get us, the weather, wild animals or Indians might.

We began preparations in earnest, and the spring of '59 saw us bidding a tearful farewell to our family and heading for New York City. It was a piecemeal journey of carriages, ferries and trains, but once there, we boarded the *Honduras*, a sleek side-wheel steamer bound for Panama. Ten days later we reached Aspinwall (now Colon), on the Caribbean side of the isthmus.

From Aspinwall we took the recently inaugurated open-air train across the narrow neck of land to the Pacific Ocean. At $25 for a 48-mile trip, it was about as expensive a train ride as I've ever been on. Still, it was better than walking through the torturous, sweltering jungle that lined the tracks over much of the distance. Panama City was an abysmal place, like a derelict with only an outside chance for redemption, and the harbour was even worse.

The *Sonora* lay alongside a dock jammed with equipment and would-be miners heading north. The prevailing mood was one of cheerful optimism, but occasionally tempers would flare in the heat and mounting excitement. Come boarding time, the gangway to the ship was awash with a current of humanity that swept us aboard. When the lines were finally cast off and the vessel made for the open ocean, there were many more passengers on board than she was designed to carry and conditions were terrible. We steamed north and west against a heavy Pacific swell to San Diego and the barren hills of southern California, then on to Monterey until at last we slipped through the Golden Gate and into the crowded harbour of San Francisco, some two weeks after departing Panama.

The city sprawled up the hillside, an agglomeration of residences, buildings of commerce and law, churches and hospitals, saloons and houses of ill repute. A hundred thousand people called San Francisco their home, which was remarkable considering that just ten years before, the population had been less than 500. The streets were teeming with people, my father and I among them, trading cash for tools and clothing in the numerous provision stores above the quays.

Two days later we were aboard the *Republic* for the final leg of the journey to Fort Victoria. The mountains became more thickly wooded the farther north we steamed, and the Oregon Territory forests were as dense as any tropical jungle. In the postdawn hours, after five days of hard steaming, we awoke to find Vancouver Island off our port bow. Slightly less than six weeks had passed since we had left Glengarry.

Our ship, though smaller than its predecessors, had too deep a draught for Victoria's inner harbour and docked instead at Esquimalt. Many passengers were transported by lighters to Victoria, and a few chose to walk, but my father and I were fortunate enough to get a carriage.

The town seethed with reports from British Columbia that prospecting along the lower reaches of the Fraser River was going mostly unrewarded. That was disappointing news to say the least, but we weren't about to turn back, and therefore wasted no time in buying our permits from the gold license office. We then hastened by the steamer *Surprise* across Georgia Strait and up the river, beyond Fort Langley to Fort Hope.

Over the summer, we panned the river bars. On Hill's Bar we cut planks from a cedar tree and built a rocker, which allowed us to wash more gravel, but did not improve its colour in the least. When winter approached, we returned to Victoria where the latest news was of a gold strike on the Similkameen River, just north of the international boundary. We wasted no time in booking passage to Olympia in Washington Territory; there we would wait for spring which would bring the opening of the mountain passes and the trail leading to south-central British Columbia.

As winter crept by, a yearning for my mother and home diluted my father's optimism and passion for gold. In March of 1860 he thought it time to put an end to his part in the adventure and set his sights once more on Canada. He only half-heartedly tried to persuade me to join him, for he could plainly see that I was determined to continue on my own. It was with considerable pride that he wished me well, and I assured him that in time, I would return to Glengarry with the wealth we had both dreamed about.

I had read in an Olympia newspaper that a Captain Collins was leading an expedition of miners and traders from Seattle to the Similkameen-Boundary country, just north of the international border.[1] Along with the possibility of gold was the incentive that whoever went along would be among the first white men to cross the Cascade Mountains from west to east. That appealed immensely to my enterprising and adventurous nature, so I quickly made my way north.

Captain Collins had a ranch of more than 600 acres about five miles outside Seattle, where I arrived on April 14, 1860. He was a notorious "Indian fighter" who seemed to want to fight Indians whether they were willing participants or not. Near the river that ran by his ranch was a blockhouse in which was hidden a piece of heavy artillery that he kept loaded with old saw teeth and rivet heads. Any unsuspecting Indian canoe that came along was doomed to be blown out of the water. He did this regardless of the mainly friendly relations between the whites and the Indians in the territory. To Collins, there were good Indians and there were bad Indians, and if they were good then it could only be because they were dead. He seemed determined to make as many of them "good" as possible. Though the captain was a man of grit, and there were many things about him I admired, his hatred of Indians and desire to kill them were distasteful in the extreme.

On April 29, 34 men and even more packhorses left Collins' ranch for British Columbia. Our route would be east across the mountains, then north through the Columbia and Okanogan river valleys.[2] It was an independent expedition, by which I mean each man had his own packhorse and supplies and would be responsible for feeding himself throughout the journey. We would travel as a group only for the safety it afforded.

As we climbed steadily east, through the timbered valleys of the foothills, the Cascades rose before us, intimidating and dangerous. It was a monotonous world of white, black, and grey: snow-draped trees and dark, rocky ledges that disappeared into the sombre clouds overhead. Despite the warming temperatures, the snow still lay thick and heavy along our path. In one spot, I measured it to be ten feet deep. At a place Collins called "Kellogg's Prairie" the horses kept sinking up to their chests in it, which severely hampered our progress. We were ordered to dismount and to dig a trench in the snow two-and-a-half feet deep, by the same width, and line it with brush and tree boughs. It acted as a crude sort of roadbed through which we passed in single file until more solid ground was reached. By then, the trench was 13 miles long. We did it all in a single day, during a spring downpour that soaked us clear to the bone, but it had to be done if we wanted to make headway.

It took us a little more than a month to cross the Cascades. Many times we came across grizzly tracks, some so large we were thankful for not having chanced upon the beasts that left them. When we finally spotted two, they were far off in the distance and wanted less to do with us than we did with them. Worse than the bears was the nighttime when the surrounding forest echoed with the hideous screeching of cougars. It was menacing enough that most of the men found it nearly impossible to sleep. To add to our hardship it rained, non-stop, for two solid weeks. Every rock and tree wept water, and everyone but me was hoarse with a cough. It was about as miserable a time as I've ever experienced. Finally, on the eastern slope we encountered some drier weather along with a rich pasturage. With the help of a warm wind and a roaring fire we were able to dry out our wet clothes while the horses enjoyed the best grazing they'd had since leaving Collins' ranch.

We followed the Yakima River for three days as it descended between banks of lofty, leafy trees and lush bushes flanked by steep, rocky bluffs and layered, folded hillsides dotted with lone pines. It was as pretty a country as could be found anywhere. The valley was eerily silent and in the late afternoon, the constant play of light and shadows on the folds and layers of the hills gave them an unearthly cast. Except for occasional glimpses of small bands of Indians, there seemed an utter absence of life.

Nevertheless, whether they could be seen or not, we often sensed the Indians' presence, as if our movement down the valley was being carefully watched.

Who could blame them if they regarded us with suspicion? We were strangers on their land and my only wish was to pass through without any trouble. I worried that Collins might want to pick a fight, and we were so few in number it would have been suicide had he done so. We rode on, fording the Yakima as we turned north toward the arid benchlands of the Columbia. "Keep your heads up," Collins said, and we did, scrutinizing every rock, tree and bush that might hide an ambush.

By mid-June, we had reached the confluence of the Okanogan and Columbia rivers. The summer heat was building steadily and now lay across our shoulders like the arm of an old friend. We were silently appreciative. None of us had forgotten that a mere two weeks before, we had been soaked to the skin and feeling as miserable as could be. Fort Okanogan was a few miles upstream on the Columbia so Captain Collins sent me and a few others to see if we could obtain some supplies and hire a boat to get the expedition across the Okanogan. We built a small raft that kept us barely afloat, crossed to the other side and walked to the fort.

John Jacob Astor originally constructed this fort in 1811, while he was building his fur empire. It was subsequently taken over by the Northwest Company and then the Hudson's Bay Company, after those two great enterprises merged in 1821. When we arrived, there were Indians encamped around the fort, doing nothing in particular, and the trader was about to abandon the place for good. Everything was packed up for a move north of the border where the HBC felt trade would be more vigorous. The trader was unwilling to open any of his packs and would therefore sell us no supplies. He did, however, have an old boat that we could use without charge. It was full of bullet holes, he said, but seaworthy nonetheless. We found it upside down on the riverbank and launched it. When it didn't sink, we drifted down river to the Okanogan, the strong current pulling the vessel at a pace even with the logs and floating debris around it.

By early evening, we'd moved all our goods to the east bank of the river, swum the horses across, and set up camp. Later, we held a meeting at which one of the members of our party requested permission to sell a ten-gallon keg of liquor to the Indians. He was transporting several of them, for it was his intention to open a saloon once we reached the mining camp. He complained that one of the kegs was giving him trouble and looked ready to spill its contents. If that happened, he stood to lose a tidy sum of money. Collins and I were vehemently opposed to such a transaction, considering it dangerous and foolhardy. Nevertheless, we had all agreed from the outset to govern ourselves democratically and when the request was put to a vote, a majority approved the sale. For the first time on that journey, I thought I might be travelling with a pack of fools.

The next morning the Indians from the fort were at our camp looking for trade goods and were happily surprised to hear there was liquor for sale. After some negotiation, they settled on a price of $60 for the keg, then headed back to the fort. Collins thought it a good idea that someone ride along behind to keep an eye on them. There was no telling what might transpire, and the captain was a cautious man. I volunteered.

At the fort, the Indians sat the keg in the middle of the yard and, using a small axe, smashed open the top with a single blow. They had two tin cups with which they ladled out the liquor, then they drank it like desert nomads trying to quench a desperate thirst. The trader, who was half French and half Indian, joined in, ignoring my warnings that trouble was brewing. There was much chatter accompanied by hard glances toward me. They wanted another keg of liquor, the trader translated, and if they didn't get it, they would fight us for it. I said they'd be getting no more liquor from me or from anyone in our party for that matter and if it meant a fight then so be it.

By then the Indians were on their third cup and began to whoop and howl. Some began plaiting the manes and tails of their horses, which usually meant only one thing: they were preparing for a fight. I rode the four miles back to Captain Collins and the men at a full gallop.

Collins said later that he was watching through his field glasses and when he saw me riding hard toward him, called out, "Run in all the horses boys, there's trouble coming." By the time I arrived, the horses had been arranged in a circle. I quickly explained to Collins what the Indians were up to and that an attack was imminent. We set to digging rifle pits among the knee-high bunchgrass, then lined the edges with our saddles and supplies. The captain, fearing that the wet weather we'd experienced might have damaged our ammunition, ordered us to shoot off half of what was in our weapons and reload them. Then we waited.

The sun climbed past its zenith. The rifle pits began to feel like a blacksmith's forge until a small breeze sprang up to ease the heat a little. Minutes crawled into hours and still there was no sign of the Indians. We were hoping they'd sobered up and changed their minds. The man who'd sold them the liquor said they shouldn't be that drunk anyway, since he'd cheated them by watering down the liquor. That piece of news didn't sit well with Collins or with me. Not only was it an underhanded deed, but we knew full well that it might serve only to make the Indians even angrier. Whatever the case, we soon discovered that they hadn't forgotten about us. Shortly after two o'clock in the afternoon, Collins detected a dust cloud in the distance and looked through his field glasses. "Here they come!" he hollered.

In all honesty, I have to say that I was feeling a little nervous about those Indians, but I was mighty impressed by them, too. They were painted and practically naked, and their horses' manes and tails had all been plaited. The white animals were dyed completely blue. I doubt I've seen finer horsemen, and the sight gave me some consternation until I saw that their only weapons were old Hudson's Bay muskets, whereas we had the very latest in rifles, shotguns, and Colt revolvers. They commenced to circle around us in single file, ducking down behind the far side of their horses and peering at us from beneath the animals' necks. Whenever they pressed closer, Collins would warn them off. I didn't worry that he would pick a fight. We were surrounded and he had more sense than to start something he couldn't finish. Even given our superior firepower, there were just too many of them. Not only that, the chief had yelled that if we whipped him and his men, there were 200 more who would be along to make sure we didn't get out of there alive.

A dozen times the Indians dared us to fire the first shot, and Collins dared them back, but no one fired. The tension was as thick as river mud. It was a hair-raising game of pure bluff in which we held the losing hand and, had cooler heads not won the day, the consequences would have been more serious than I care to think about. Those Indians whooped and hollered and circled us for five long hours before deciding that either we were not to be trifled with, or we simply weren't worth the bother any more, that they'd been given all the liquor they were going to get. In small groups they began to disperse until all that remained was a trampled circle, like a noose, around 34 jumpy men who were beginning to believe once again in tomorrow.

By that time, the sun was taking its leave and the land was turning purple. There was much nervous speculation about how things might have turned out, even some bravado, then a profound silence settled over the men as thoughts turned inward. Stars drifted across a moonless sky and the evening spoke well of summer. Yet it left me feeling strangely remote from my companions. I realized for the first time that, as close as we may stand with our fellow human beings during perilous times, there is much we have to face alone.

We stayed in our pits for the rest of the night, our weapons at our sides, just in case the Indians returned. But all stayed quiet, and in the morning there were no Indians to be seen anywhere, only the empty, undulating country spanning the distance before us.

We picked our way north, up the Okanogan Valley, beside the river lined with willows and cottonwoods. Forty miles north of the Columbia, we cut through McLaughlin Canyon to a rich tableland of grassy hills and secluded draws where the going was about as easy as we'd had it. We saw no one, and a week later, without further incident, arrived in Rock Creek, three miles north of the international boundary. Collins called everyone together and after making a short speech, officially disbanded the expedition.

It was a blistering hot country we'd come to, smelling of pine resin, sagebrush, and parched earth. There wasn't an ounce of moisture in the air and the entire valley felt like a forest fire about to ignite.

There were many claims already staked up and down the length of the narrow valley and most of them had only begun to be worked. The average claim was paying about $30 a day per man while the two discovery claims were each paying $50, which was pretty good money for those days. Even so, a lot of gold was being overlooked because many of the miners, myself included, were greenhorns who didn't know about all the places in which gold lurks. That was something we wouldn't learn until years later. Regardless, no one ever really knew exactly how much gold was being taken out of the ground because it never stayed around long enough to be tallied up. Most of it disappeared south of the border. I believe that by the time the rush ended, it was reported that Rock Creek had yielded about $250,000 in gold, but in my opinion, that figure was ridiculously low.

I found only limited prospects in Rock Creek, so when my resources began to dwindle I took a job as customs officer at Osoyoos. I did not find it the least bit appealing. My life was in constant danger from the blackguards roaming along the border, who seemed to prefer killing me to paying customs dues. Barely a week went by without one of them trying to put a bullet through me or my deputy, a young man I knew from Canada West named Peter Gibson. Still, I was more annoyed than frightened. I didn't fear death as much as I feared a wasted life.

After all, death waits for all of us with open arms, and life is but a pathway to its grasp. But it behooves us as free-thinking men to at least choose the path that we take. I had come west for adventure and to make a fortune, not to make $250 a month in obscurity as a government employee. What's more, the promise I had made to my father had been nagging at me lately and my soul was feeling more than a little restless. Then thunderous news came from Victoria that caused a great stirring in my chest. A major gold strike — 200 ounces a day — had been made on Antler Creek in a region up north called "Cariboo."

The story was that a man named "Doc" Keithley and his partner, Isaiah Diller, had found good signs of colour on a creek running into Cariboo Lake that now bears Keithley's name.[3] Like any gold-bearing creek it was soon over-worked, so Keithley and three companions went exploring. They found the source of another creek and followed its course. It was as if deer came there to die for they saw antlers strewn along the banks. Farther down, beyond a small canyon, they found what they'd been looking for and could scarcely believe their eyes. Nuggets of gold shone in the shallows and all they needed to do at first was reach into the cold water and scoop them out.

I tendered my resignation immediately.

I was told that there was a great demand for pack trains in Lillooet, and that if I purchased some horses to resell there, it might prove to be a good investment. Using most of my savings I bought a hundred horses from around the Osoyoos area at $40 a head. I was about $600 short of the cash required for the deal, but was able to work out an agreement with Big Chief Tonasket of the Okanagan Indians. He'd made some money running the Hudson's Bay Company's horse ranges and selling riding equipment to them, and wanted in on the investment. He would loan me the money on the condition that he was allowed to accompany me on the journey and get paid a daily wage at the same time. That suited me just fine. Tonasket was a powerful man who was held in high regard by all, whites and Indians alike. His authority extended to both sides of the border and it was said that he could whip any three men at one time. I reckoned it would be to my advantage to have him along should I encounter hostile Indians on the way.

During the spring of '61, I set off for Lillooet with Tonasket and another Indian to assist us. We were soon joined by a Mr. Jim Rowlands who had driven 150 head of cattle up from The Dalles, in the Oregon Territory, and was on his way to sell them in Cariboo. He also had an Indian assisting him. The horses and cattle drove well together and we moved along at a good pace, heading north through the vast aridness and heat of the Okanagan Valley.

We made Okanagan Lake without any serious mishaps, but near a place later called Peachland, I was off rounding up some stray horses when I heard the chief roaring like an angry bull. I spurred my horse toward the sound of his voice and rode head-long into a duel between Tonasket and Rowlands. They were standing several paces apart with guns raised and pointed at each other. The chief was calling, "One, two ..." and I was crying, "Don't shoot! Don't shoot!" In an instant that passed more like an eternity I was off my horse before it stopped and jumped Rowlands, wresting the pistol from his hand. He was trembling over every inch of his body and to this day, I have never seen a man as visibly shaken as he was. Tonasket, on the other hand, was as cool as a mountain stream.

I demanded to know what the fight was about and Rowlands complained that Tonasket had tried to set fire to his bull. Apparently, the bull had gone lame, lain down, and stubbornly refused to get up. The chief knew a tried-and-true way to get an animal up and moving. He gathered together some dry grass and placed it around the bull, then set fire to it. I thought that to be an unusually cruel act and told him so. I also said that it was not his bull and therefore he had no right to interfere.

The chief turned his anger on me, threatening to quit and take his horses with him. I asserted that I would not permit such an action, that we had an agreement and we would both stick to it, regardless of the circumstances. Suddenly, Tonasket jumped me. I was a good two inches shorter than he, but weighed nearly 200 pounds, none of which was wasted on fat. I was able to maintain my balance and, despite his great strength, wrestle him to the ground. Once I had him flat on his back, the fight went out of him and he relinquished his hold on me. I took away his gun and said he'd get it back when things cooled down a bit. He was furious and I knew I was going to have to keep my eye on him.

That night Rowlands and I sat up watching the horses. We both suspected that Tonasket would probably try stealing off with them. Not long before daybreak, we caught him trying to do just that. I warned him in simple language about what would happen should he try anything so foolish again. He was still angry, although most of his anger was directed toward Rowlands. But he heeded my warning and restrained himself by avoiding his new-made enemy whenever possible.

We continued north, along the old Hudson's Bay Company trail to Fort Kamloops, then west, following a difficult trail above Kamloops Lake and the Thompson River. By mid-August, we had reached Hat Creek, where it joins the Bonaparte River.

The following morning Rowlands and I went our separate ways as he turned his herd north along the Bonaparte — a mighty sorry excuse for a river — toward the goldfields. As soon as he was out of sight, Tonasket returned to his old self and I felt safe enough to give him back his pistol. We went west along Hat Creek, then veered off between the steep walls of Marble Canyon, past some picturesque lakes and into Pavilion Valley. We reached Lillooet four days later, and there were so many people, wagons and animals crowding the town I could barely move sideways.

It was our good fortune not to have lost a single horse over the entire journey and, soon after we arrived, I sold the entire herd for an average of $150 per head. I paid the chief the money owed him and the daily wages we'd agreed upon, then threw in a fine gift as well. He was more than happy, and we parted as good friends. After paying our assistant the wages that he had earned, I was left with a tidy profit of $10,000.

I had never had so much money in my life. But money was as ubiquitous as the pine trees around Lillooet, handed over eagerly by men bound for the creeks to other men just as eager to take it from them. As someone later said, a miner was little more than the "means of conveying money into another person's pockets." Most of them were like the nomadic tribes who move through the desert from oasis to oasis for the sustenance of water, only they moved from creek to creek sustained by the quest for gold. They could no more do anything about it than a butterfly could stop shedding its cocoon. Their nature meant

Marble Canyon. (COURTESY OF BC ARCHIVES C-09841)

that anyone with a good head for business could parlay earnings into a small fortune, as many did — as I did. Yet for the miners, the stakes were much higher. They believed there were bigger fortunes awaiting them. They believed in Eldorado. And in those days, I counted myself among them.

The journey north to Antler took me through Williams Lake where there was another indication of the easy money flying about Cariboo back then — a high-stakes horse race. I arrived just as the contest was about to get under way. Only two horses were running and the wager between the owners alone was near $70,000!

Now I don't mean to imply that everybody had that kind of money to throw around. In reality, many were dead broke by the time they reached the creeks. But there were a number of men who were financially comfortable, thanks to the miners, and I was fortunate enough to be one of them. Yet I had not forgotten my father's words, and loaned money whenever I felt a man was deserving of it. If he struck it rich, I knew I'd get my money back, and if he didn't, well, it was an investment in the common good.

Upon reaching Antler Creek in early September I bought into a claim and purchased a building in town for $4,000. Antler town was a booming proposition then, with nearly a

Lillooet in 1865, looking nowhere near as busy as it was during Stevenson's visit. (COURTESY OF BC ARCHIVES A-09064)

dozen saloons, several general stores, a couple of blacksmith's shops, and even a butcher shop. If a man had the money, he could buy pretty much anything he wanted, even a woman if he wasn't very particular.

That was the fall of '61, near the end of the mining season. Most of the miners were pulling out until spring, to winter in Victoria, so on November 3, under a light snowfall, I left for the coast with three companions. The snow continued as we worked our way south, across the plateau, but it wasn't deep enough to make walking difficult. Besides, I preferred it to the mosquitoes and flies of summer, especially along the often-swampy trail between Antler and Hat Creek where they were particularly nasty. Below Hat Creek was new territory for me. Once we crossed the Thompson River at Cook and Kimball's Ferry (later Spence's Bridge), the trail was as rugged and dangerous as anything in my experience. In places, the barren mountains plunged straight into the river, which raged by in a stunning green-and-white torrent. For 20 miles the trail rose and fell precipitously, and each footstep seemed more perilous than the last. At Lytton the snow had increased with uncommon fury until it lay nearly five feet deep. We were held up in a roadhouse there for an entire day, waiting for a break in the weather.

The next morning we left early, under a promising sky. The terrible beauty of the Thompson, clear and clean, pouring into the silt-laden Fraser, was breathtaking. For a short time the two rivers ran side by side, down the same channel, as if they were vying for it. But the Fraser was soon triumphant and easily swallowed up its rival, as it will most things that venture too close.

Despite the improvement in the weather, the walking only increased in difficulty. The snow had crusted and since we had no snowshoes, it was especially hard on the leader, who had to break trail. The first step was like falling into a hole up to your waist, and the next was like trying to step out, only to fall into another one. We struggled along in single file, lifting our legs high to clear the snow, like some kind of grotesque march, and each mile felt like ten. Even though we took turns leading, all three of us were as spent as old pennies by day's end.

Down river, the trail ascended quite steeply up the flank of a high mountain and then fell off alarmingly on the far side. To this day, I can't say whether it was worse climbing up the one side or slipping and sliding down the other. I can, however, say with absolute certainty that we were all grateful when it flattened out along the benches near Boston Bar and the going got a little easier. Yet, just to prove that nothing's ever free, there were deep ravines that had to be crossed on slippery logs. We slithered across those on our bellies, and thought that was bad until we entered Black Canyon.

The trail, if one could call it that, was primitive at best and in places clung so precariously to the rock walls that we were forced to our hands and knees for safety. With every movement forward, it seemed there was only a hair's breadth between life and death. The river boiled down the canyon, dirty brown, sometimes so close that the roar was deafening, at other times so far below my feet that I dared not look down for even a second, for fear that it would pull me to my death. At Hell's Gate, the cleft was so narrow that a stone could be thrown to the other side. The river gushed through the slit in the rocks with such terrifying power that the mere thought of it made my head spin for days afterwards.

Hell's Gate, Fraser Canyon, 1867. (COURTESY OF BC ARCHIVES A-03874)

A few miles downstream we came upon the Indian burial grounds at Spuzzum and crossed over the Fraser on the new suspension bridge. The trail cut away from the river there and it was a blessed relief to leave that torrent behind for a while. The silence was blissful until we joined up with it again, but by then we were near our destination and secure in the knowledge that we would arrive safely. We reached Yale on December 5, having taken ten long, gruelling days to go only 57 miles down river from Lytton. Never had the threshold to civilization looked more inviting.

Yale, being located at the end of the navigable part of the Fraser River, was crowded with travellers waiting for the next steamer to depart for New Westminster. I was lucky to find a

room in town, and waited nine days before the *Onward* departed on her last trip to the coast for the season.

On December 14, a day bitter with cold, all those departing
on the *Onward* were quick to board her, the fare to New
Westminster being $13. She was a sternwheeler with a draft so
shallow that it was said if anyone fell overboard they'd probably raise a cloud of dust. William Irving was her captain. He
was a competent man, who only a few months before had managed to escape with his life after the steamer *Fort Yale* blew up
a mile or two above Hope.

He was a passenger on that ill-fated vessel and had just left
the pilothouse after a visit with her captain, Smith Jamieson,
when the boiler blew it to smithereens. Indians arrived in canoes
to take the survivors to shore, but Irving remained on board
what was left of the *Fort Yale* to try and beach her. She ended

*Yale in 1865. All steamboat travel on the lower Fraser River ended here,
the gateway to Cariboo.* (COURTESY OF BC ARCHIVES A-00902)

The steamer Onward *at Yale, with Captain Irving in the wheelhouse.*
(COURTESY OF BC ARCHIVES A-00102)

up grounding herself on a gravel bar not far below Hope. Parts of the vessel were found a half-mile from the explosion, but Jamieson had vanished without a trace. He was the third brother to die in a steamer accident, but not, I regret to say, the last. Four months later, the steamer *Cariboo* was leaving Victoria harbour when she blew sky high, killing the captain, Archibald Jamieson, and the second engineer, James Jamieson. They were the last of five brothers who had left their home in Scotland to find a new life but found eternity instead.

The river was freezing hard and fast as we came alongside the dock at New Westminster. The next morning, the *Otter*, which was to take us to Victoria, had to be cut from the ice before she could move an inch. It was about an hour and a half before we could get under way, but by nightfall, we had arrived safely in Victoria. Three weeks later, the Fraser River was frozen hard all the way up to Hope, and was closed to traffic for more than two months.

Chapter Three

CAMERON WAS VISIBLY impressed with my résumé, commenting that I had accomplished much for so young a man. That wasn't anything I'd given much thought to, for it seems to me that life isn't much more than a series of opportunities that we can either let slip by, or grab on to. I have always preferred the latter course.

My story had taken us through a few whiskeys and we both felt in need of a walk to clear our heads. It was late afternoon and the weather was much improved, made all the more agreeable by my companion. We left the Boomerang and walked up Chancery Lane to Government Street, then crossed to the south side of Fort Street, past Searby's drugstore. The wooden crosswalk at the intersection was sagging badly in the middle and half-covered with muddy water, but it was drier than the street so we crossed over on it anyway, and walked east on Fort. Our footsteps thudded on the wooden sidewalk as a mud-spattered carriage and a similarly bedecked water cart clattered by in quick succession. To our left, hitching posts lined the curb, while to our right were shops with overhead signs proclaiming

Looking north along Government Street, with the Little Brown Jug Saloon on the right. (COURTESY OF BC ARCHIVES A-03453)

their business: a tinsmith, an ironmonger, even the library. But I scarcely paid attention to where we were walking as Cameron related the events that had brought him to Victoria.

He had grown up with a head full of dreams, he said, and couldn't remember when he first became aware that dreams of adventure and fortune were among them. Perhaps they had always been there, nurturing a restless spirit and stirring his soul, pushing him inexorably toward the day when he would abandon farm life to go in search of something better. He had long grown tired of working on his uncle's farm near Summerstown, in Glengarry County, and getting paid only a modest wage into the bargain. It didn't matter that farming had been in his family for generations; he, John Angus Cameron, would never be content with a pastoral existence. Consequently, when news arrived that gold had been found in great quantities in California, it was news he'd been born to hear.

What's more, he was not getting any younger. In 1852, he was about to turn 32, and if he expected to marry his 19-year-old fiancée, Sophia Groves, then he would need to improve his prospects considerably. She was the daughter of Nathan Groves, a well-respected veteran of the War of 1812, who had fought in the Battle of Lundy's Lane and was also a farmer in the township of Cornwall. Cameron thought she deserved something more than a life as a farmer's wife, and if that was all he could offer her then perhaps it would be best for both of them if he remained a bachelor. So that spring he said goodbye to his family and told Sophia that when he returned to marry her, it would be as a wealthy man.

Fort Street. The building on the left houses Searby's drugstore.
(Courtesy of BC Archives A-02997)

He knew that getting to California would be no small task, and began to have an inkling just how big it was shortly after his ship, the *Honduras*, left New York for Panama. The sea was restless, and huge swells rolling down the coast soon had him heaving over the rails. When he finally found his sea legs, they were wobbly at best. Five days out of New York the dark green hump of Cuba rose on the blue horizon and soon they were slipping through the narrows and dropping anchor in Havana harbour.

A swarm of native canoes, filled with all manner of fruit to sell, attached themselves to the side of the *Honduras* like pilotfish to a shark. He'd never seen oranges so big, nor tasted any so juicy. Unable to sleep below because of the heat, he spent the night on the promenade deck and awoke at dawn to the sound of the vessel making her way out to sea. A fresh breeze from the north whipped the flag of Spain flying high over El Morro, the castle guarding the entrance to Havana harbour. As the sun rose on the horizon, the *Honduras* muscled her way from the sheltered waters into a good chop and turned westward for Yucatan Channel.

Sailing past some of those Caribbean islands momentarily made Cameron think he need go no farther, for this was surely Paradise itself: the palm-fringed beaches of white coral sand washed by azure water were almost as alluring as the thought of fabulous wealth. But it grew so hot he could barely stand it, even with the movement of the ship and the steady breeze across the weather deck. Then he came down with a bad case of mouth boils — a malady many of his fellow passengers also suffered — that did not improve his disposition a whit. By the time he got to Aspinwall his Utopian delusions had withered under the intense tropical sun.

And he certainly hadn't reckoned on the rugged trail across the isthmus. The railroad had not yet been built so he had to hire a *bungo*, the local name for a dugout canoe, and a native guide to take him up the Chagres River to the foot trail that led to Panama City. He bargained hard and managed to get the asking price of $50 down to $25, but when he returned to the canoe after getting his supplies, it was gone, along with his money. He had to pay an additional $30 for another guide, but this time he made sure never to let the man out of his sight.

It was a 40-mile journey upriver against swift water, much of it lined with impenetrable jungle on both sides. If he had thought that summer days along the St. Lawrence River could be hot, humid and mosquito infested, he soon discovered they were no match for that sweltering jungle. The mosquitoes were ferocious and malarial, and there were swarms of other insects capable of inflicting even worse damage. When it rained it was a deluge and the thunderstorms were stupendous. He had a rubber blanket to protect himself from the downpours, but it was like a sweathouse underneath and he got soaked anyway. At night the native guide slept on shore while Cameron, fearing alligators, slept in the bungo. After three blistering hot days of paddling, they arrived at Las Cruces and the foot trail leading to Panama City. He might have felt better about leaving the river behind if it had improved his situation, but it didn't.

First there was the "hotel" that was nothing more than a stable crammed with makeshift bunks. He paid a dollar for the privilege of sleeping with an army of lice and bedbugs, and men who smelled worse than he did. Then he bargained poorly and paid dearly for a mule that was a sorry excuse for a beast of burden. It was so emaciated he feared it wouldn't make it to the edge of the village let alone the Pacific Ocean. Nevertheless, it cost him $20. Once on the trail, the heat beneath the canopy of trees was debilitating and to make matters even more insufferable, the ground had been turned into a bog by the countless gold-seekers preceding him. The mule spent much of the trip knee-deep in mud and sank up to its chest twice, forcing Cameron to dismount and lead the poor creature to firmer ground. When he finally reached Panama City, he was filthy, soaked and saddle-sore, and so relieved to be there that he scarcely noticed how dismal and shabby a place it truly was. He set up his tent among hundreds of others on the edge of town and discovered to his horror that the camp was rife with yellow fever, malaria, dysentery and cholera. He was glad he'd brought a generous supply of brandy with him to bolster his immune system.

When he arrived at the docks to board the steamer to San Francisco, he thanked his lucky stars that the ticket he'd bought back in New York included a berth. There was a fierce competition under way and men were bidding up to $1,000 for one. When all the berths were gone, every nook and cranny was sold as if they offered the comfort of a king's bed. The vessel became so overcrowded that having a berth really wasn't much of an advantage, especially in steerage where Cameron was quartered. There was scarcely enough room to take a deep breath let alone turn around, and it was an excruciatingly uncomfortable and dangerous journey north. He didn't know which made him more nauseated, the rolling ocean or the smell of vomit and excrement. It was a way of sea travel that some deemed worse than a Siberian prison, with a risk of drowning added for good measure. When he disembarked at San

Francisco, he felt as if he'd just been given a reprieve from Hell and passage into Heaven.

But those feelings were short-lived. When he reached the California creeks they looked like a war zone, with endless tree stumps, muddy streams, huge mounds of dirt and sludge-filled sluice holes as deep as bomb craters. If there was a stone left unturned it was going to require much determination to find it. The sheer number of people Cameron encountered astonished him: thousands upon thousands of them, in endless variety, for it seemed every race on the planet was represented there. The camps were rough places where a man could buy whiskey or a woman, or into a high-stakes card game, more easily than good grub. And with the exception of the whiskey, none of it was cheap. For a moment, he felt like reversing his footsteps until he was safely back in Glengarry, but then he thought of Sophia and knew that wasn't an option. So he ignored his languor from the long and arduous journey, and immediately went to work to find his fortune in the much-abused creeks of California.

He toiled for six years, much harder than he'd ever had to work back home on the farm. But he loved placer mining with a passion he'd never experienced before, for every displacement of a rock, or swirl of a pan, every shovelful of dirt into the sluice box held the promise of untold riches, and that was something that farm labour could never offer. Before long, his efforts were rewarded. He found gold, not a streak, but enough to cover his expenses and then some.

That was the high point for Cameron in California. After that, things did not go at all well for him. His luck turned suddenly and went racing off in the opposite direction like a horse scenting the barn. He bought a worthless mine, then spent most of the rest of his money constructing a long flume to it. In his eternal optimism, he believed that even though this claim had been worked over hard, its true value had not yet been tapped. He was wrong. The mine had definitely petered out and offered up nothing more than colourless dirt.

In 1858, when news of the Fraser River strikes reached his ears, he sold what assets he could and went north. There, his luck changed dramatically. By the winter of '59 he'd made $20,000 and decided that his prospects were as good as they'd ever been and it was time to return to Glengarry County and claim Sophia for his wife. Provided, of course, she would still have him. Their separation had been long and communication between them scant, and he prayed that she awaited his return as eagerly as he did.

The journey to California was pleasant, made all the more so by a full gold poke. In San Francisco, he booked passage south on the *Sonora* and when he arrived in Panama City, the size of the crowd of miners waiting to board the vessel for her return trip north astonished him. And of course, he had no idea that my father and I were among that crowd, just as we did not know he was one of the ship's passengers.

Once back in Glengarry County, Cameron wasted no time in confirming Sophia's assent to the marriage. Though he wouldn't have thought it possible, she'd grown even lovelier in his absence. All the dangers, all the hard work it had taken him to reach this moment were justified by the first glimpse of her face. And though Sophia saw in his a more worldly look, it was still the one that had been on her mind since the day they parted. She could scarcely believe that he was home at last. They set about organizing their wedding, a large affair, which took place in the Presbyterian church in Cornwall. Cameron was in a daze over his good luck.

He spent some of his money putting up new buildings on his parents' farm outside Lancaster, a dozen miles down the St. Lawrence from Cornwall, and buying a house nearby that pleased Sophia. She soon became pregnant and in early January of 1861 gave birth to a beautiful daughter they named Mary Isabella Alice. By late spring, word of gold for the taking in the creeks of Cariboo had stunned Canada West and Cameron grew restless. He knew in his bones that there was a fortune out there waiting for him, but he had to convince Sophia of that and persuade her to make the long journey to the west coast with him.

The Camerons on their wedding day in 1859. Sophia was 27 years old, and Cameron was 39. (COURTESY OF BC ARCHIVES A-01158)

The three of them, he insisted, should be on their way with as much haste as possible, before the gold disappeared into some-one else's poke. She was swept away by her husband's enthusi-asm as much as by his forceful nature and, much to her sur-prise and displeasure, found herself agreeing.

Though it was stretching his finances to the limit, Cameron had enough money to obtain first- class berths for himself and Sophia as far as California. He wanted her and Mary to be as comfortable as possible, but knew he would probably have to make compromises in San Francisco.

The trip down to Aspinwall was pure agony. The sea was wild and frenzied, and more than once Cameron wondered if the vessel could withstand the beating she was taking day after day. Sophia was terrified, but instructed her husband that should the ship founder, he was to concentrate his efforts on saving their daughter. They limped into Havana three days late and were delayed there for repairs. By the time they reached Panama, what was typically a nine-day journey had taken them two-and-a-half weeks.

Fortunately, the train was now running across the isthmus, but in Panama City they experienced even further delays because of the huge throngs of miners clamouring for a berth north. In the meantime, little Mary Isabella Alice had come down with a fever.

They stopped over in San Francisco to take her to a doctor who diagnosed the problem as a common ague, possibly malar-ial, and prescribed some quinine. It didn't help the child a bit.

In February of 1862, the Camerons boarded the steamer *Brother Jonathan*, bound for Victoria. He was so short of cash by then that he couldn't afford the $50 cost of a cabin and had to book steerage. The vessel was crammed to the pilothouse with 750 passengers, most of them harbouring the same dreams as Cameron. Upon their arrival in Esquimalt harbour, the couple had $40 to their name and a seriously sick child on their hands.

Chapter Four

CAMERON AND I walked on, up past Christ Church Cathedral, and stopped at the Quadra Street cemetery to pay our respects to the Jamieson brothers. We had not known them, of course, but their tragedy was felt by the entire town and it would have been a cold heart indeed that did not allow its owner to pause for at least a moment.

I had been doing a lot of thinking as my new friend related his story, and before he finished, I had reached a decision. Not only had he accumulated an enviable knowledge of placer mining that would be useful, he was as hardy as the Highland stock from which he was descended, and that was a trait I much admired. He was forthright in manner and freely expressed his opinions, and though I did not necessarily agree with all that he said, I certainly appreciated his zeal. That, too, would be useful. He openly admitted possessing a stubborn streak that would put a mule to shame, although I wouldn't find out till later how much of an understatement that was. In some respects he reminded me of my father, although his sense of humour was certainly wanting. In fact, my father's words were foremost

Fort Street, mud and all, looking much as it did during Cameron's and Stevenson's walk. The building that housed the library is just up from Broad Street, which can be seen near the centre of the picture. Christ Church Cathedral is perched on the hill to the right. (COURTESY OF BC ARCHIVES A-02999)

in my mind as I considered a proposition that I would make to Cameron. I knew beyond a doubt that he would be reliable, that he was exactly the man I needed for the task I had in mind.

On our way back to the hotel, I laid out my plan. It had been my intention to return to Antler with a pack train of supplies that I would sell there out of my recently purchased building. The profits from that venture would help finance my mining operation. However, to do that I would have to wait until the snow had melted sufficiently on the Cariboo trails to allow horses to get through. Also, since there were 2,000 miners anxious to get to the creeks, and a limited number of packers to get them there, I might have to wait my turn and would therefore arrive later than was desirable. On the other hand, if I entrusted that job to Cameron, I could leave sooner, be on the creeks in time for the arrival of the first packers and sell their merchandise out of my building for a commission. Such an arrangement would benefit the packers, particularly if I gave them an advancement against future money so that they could return to the coast without delay to acquire more goods, and it would benefit me, for I would take ten percent on everything I sold. Then, when the Camerons arrived with my goods, the profits would be prodigious. To this end, I offered to stake Cameron to $2,000 worth of provisions for himself that he would bring up by pack train along with my merchandise and mining equipment. He jumped at the proposition as could only a man with a rapidly thinning billfold. At the Royal Hotel we shook hands on our new partnership and arranged to meet the following morning when I would take him to the Hudson's Bay Company store and introduce him to the trader.

At breakfast, the Camerons were conspicuous by their absence. I ran into them afterward as they were descending the narrow, bannistered staircase to the lobby. They both looked drained. Their daughter's condition had worsened overnight and they were fearful of losing her. Cameron asked to delay our meeting for an hour while they took the child to see a doctor. Upon their return, it was apparent that little had been done to alleviate their concern, but the doctor had prescribed some medicine and they were hopeful it would work.

Cameron and I went directly to the Hudson's Bay warehouse, a big barn of a building on Wharf Street, where I introduced him to the chief trader with whom we discussed our plans at length. Eventually, we reached an agreement that Cameron would receive $2,000 worth of goods for which I would stand security. My friend was euphoric. Less than 24 hours earlier he

The Hudson's Bay Company warehouse in Victoria in 1862.
(COURTESY OF BC ARCHIVES D-02015)

had felt in desperate straits, wondering what fate would bring, and now he could scarcely believe his good fortune.

"You'll not regret this deed, Stevenson," he enthused, clapping me soundly on the shoulder. "One day it will stand us both in good stead."

I felt Cameron's optimism in that touch, as much as I felt my own, which was as certain as rain on this sodden coast.

We met again the next day and made a detailed list of the supplies we would need for our venture. It included everything from nails to candles: in short, anything that a miner might purchase to make his quest for gold a trifle easier. Some smaller items had to be purchased at other stores and so we made the rounds, arguing good-naturedly over this and that, as excited and plump with enthusiasm as two men can be. This cheerfulness was to be short-lived, however, tempered by the most tragic and devastating news.

Shortly after daybreak on Monday morning, a loud knocking startled me awake. I quickly pulled on my trousers and swung open the door. It was Cameron, still in his nightclothes, and the look in his eyes made my heart leap.

"Come quickly," he said. "It's Mary."

I followed him back down the short hallway to his room. An oil lamp on the washstand and the half-light of morning through the window cast shadows on Sophia's face as she sat on the edge of the bed, slowly rocking back and forth, holding the lifeless form of their daughter in her arms. The little girl had succumbed to the fever while her parents slept beside her. To this day, I see Sophia's face as clearly as I did then, a study in pain and grief, as if the responsibility for every mishap in the world was hers and hers alone. It was all I could do to keep from enfolding her in my arms. Cameron did his best to provide comfort, but was so grief-stricken himself that I thought I would never again see a more pathetic sight. But I was more wrong than I could imagine.

I hurried down to the lobby and found Mr. Wilcox, the hotel's owner, already on duty at the desk. He advised me not to worry, that he would send for the undertaker. Soon a serious-looking, bearded man, who introduced himself as Mr. Richard Lewis, arrived. He conferred with Mr. Wilcox who kindly allowed him to use a room in the rear of the hotel to prepare Mary for burial.

The afternoon was wet and windy with sombre clouds overhead, although a clearing sky showed promise beyond the hills to the west. At half past two o'clock, Mr. Lewis returned to the Royal with his funeral wagon, and the tiny coffin containing Mary's remains was placed in the back. A small procession splashed along the muddy streets to the cemetery on Quadra Street. The Camerons were Presbyterian, and though there was no church in Victoria at the time, Mr. Lewis was able to locate a minister, the Reverend John Hall. He presided over the grave, reading from the Psalms, his strong voice slicing through the incessant wind. "Earth to earth, ashes to ashes and dust to dust," he intoned, and little Mary Isabella Alice Cameron was lowered to her rest while tears streaked the faces of her parents and a burst of sunshine washed the cemetery. She had been on this earth only 14 short months. Too soon to be taken away, the Reverend said, but God tends to our fate in his own way.

Mary's death was an immense blow to the Camerons. They blamed themselves for exposing her to risks that might have been avoided had they stayed in Glengarry County. But there is no profit in such thinking and I gently told them so. I encouraged them to look ahead rather than behind, for even though much can be learned from the past, dwelling there has more than its share of pitfalls. I began to wonder, however, if their despair was going to be more than they could bear. During her worst moments, Sophia would insist that somehow John must try to raise the money needed for them to catch the first steamer bound anywhere out of Victoria, as long as their ultimate destination was Canada and home.

I offered them the cost of the tickets in the form of a loan, but Cameron was determined not to return home empty-handed. He refused my offer. He had come this far and he would see it through. Sophia was his wife and so would she. They would find consolation, he insisted, in the fact that Sophia was with child again and would give birth sometime in the fall. Slowly, they managed to pick themselves up, Cameron more quickly than Sophia, and were soon able to cope with life's daily routines. Then they began busying themselves in preparation for the long journey to British Columbia's interior.

After a good storm at the beginning of March, the weather had warmed and spring flowers were beginning to show their colour. It was apparent from our vantage point that the snow was beginning to retreat on the Olympic Mountains across Juan de Fuca's strait. Even the newspaper was no longer carrying advertisements selling "Fresh Fraser River ice," and by the middle of the month the river was completely clear. Miners were packing up and leaving, heedless of warnings in the newspapers that because of the prolonged winter, provisions were low at the roadhouses and the trails were still thick with snow. It was recommended that everyone wait until at least the middle of April before trying to get to the creeks. That meant the mining season would be starting later than usual.

The news dampened no one's enthusiasm and the streets became busy with people buying provisions and trying out pack animals. There were mules and horses for sale on street corners, and there was even an auction for camels: there were 25 of these beasts in San Francisco, waiting for the highest bidder to snap them up. The advertisement bragged that each one could pack up to 500 pounds, and their long legs would allow them easy passage through deep snow. Not only that, they would be perfect for the desert-like summers in southern Cariboo as they could go days without water. The editor of the

The camels were referred to as the "Dromedary Express," a misnomer, for they were actually Bactrian, or two-humped camels. They were so despised by other packers that a petition was raised to ban them. Within two years many were released into the wild to become feral, and six were taken to the ranch of one of their owners. The last one died at Grande Prairie in 1905.

(COURTESY OF BC ARCHIVES A-00347)

British Colonist thought the whole idea of using camels absurd and predicted that the next thing they'd be doing would be sending freight across the water on the backs of whales, with passengers riding inside the mammals "*à la* Jonah."

Still, an undaunted freighter in Lillooet bought the animals for $300 each. He would soon discover that not only were they unsuited to the rugged British Columbian terrain and climate, they also smelled to high heaven and bit or kicked anything that moved around them. Indeed, they hadn't been off the steamer at Port Douglas for five minutes before one of them kicked a mule to death.

Soon criers roamed the streets shouting the departure time of the first steamboat to New Westminster. Restlessness was building in the miners to the point of rowdiness. So anxious were they to get under way, back to their claims or to stake one, that often tempers would flare up into fights. One afternoon as I was walking up Yates Street, trying to shake off the lethargy caused by a more than adequate lunch, I saw a large commotion around the corner of Langley Street. In front of the Confederate Saloon the police were breaking up a fight between two Americans who had brought the War Between the States to the streets of Victoria. (Given the large American population it was only natural that there would be sympathizers from both sides of the war. Some saloons and shops went so far as to hang either the Stars and Stripes or the Confederate flag out front, depending on their leanings. One group of men even had Jefferson Davis' written approval to become privateers and rob the gold ships leaving Victoria! Thanks to the sharp ear of a Yankee sympathizer they were caught before the plan got off the ground.)

The anxiety to move on increased even further when the newspaper reported that smallpox had come to town, arriving as an unwanted passenger on a steamer out of San Francisco. Vaccinations were made available to those who wanted them, but I was young and healthy and was not worried about contracting such a disease. And even though I'd led a rather leisurely life over the past three and a half months, I was still fit and ready to move on. I began my own preparations in earnest.

I had no intention of waiting until mid-April to leave. It made good business sense to be on the creeks ahead of everyone else so on Tuesday morning, April 1, I was up as day was breaking in the eastern sky. A quick glance out the window was enough to show that March, which had come in like a lion, had left meek as a lamb. Wharf Street was just beginning to show signs of life as a freight wagon trundled by, bound, I expect, for the Hudson's Bay Company wharf. After a hearty breakfast I thanked the Wilcoxes for their kind service and was on the wharf myself at eight o'clock. I had my packboard, filled with the supplies needed for the journey, and to it was tied a pair of snowshoes. I would never again be caught in that country without them.

This was the first steamer of the season to New Westminster and the wharf was packed with passengers and well-wishers, most of the former being miners who were as heedless as I was of the newspaper's warnings. Everyone was in high spirits, the air so charged with excitement that one old-timer cried he'd not seen anything like it since the spring of '58. Reverend Garret, that old Episcopalian proselytizer, whose presence on the wharf could usually be counted on, was standing on a barrel that served as a pulpit, waving his arms and shouting verses from the Bible over the noise of the crowd and a small choir singing hymns, determined to win as many souls as possible before they were lost forever in the wilds of Cariboo.

The steamer *Otter* lay alongside the wharf. The crew had stowed the last of her cargo below and the gangway was being made ready for boarding. I bade farewell to the Camerons, who had come to see me off, and received their assurances that we would be reunited on the creeks. I boarded the ship and at ten minutes past nine o'clock the lines were cast off amid cheers and shouts of "Good luck!" and "God speed!" while the singing of the choir rose to the heavens. The *Otter* inched into the harbour, shuddered as she came about, and increased speed. We crept past Laurel Point and Ogden Point, picking up even more speed as we steamed into the choppy waters of the strait. Ten hours later we were docking at New Westminster or, as it had been appropriately nicknamed, "Stumpville."

New Westminster during the 1860s — a town with more stumps than people.
(COURTESY OF BC ARCHIVES A-03330)

Chapter Five

O NCE ON THE mainland, there were two ways to get to Cariboo and both began by paddlewheeler at New Westminster. The Douglas and Lillooet route went up the Fraser and Harrison rivers, then up Harrison Lake to Port Douglas. A 30-mile wagon road led to Lillooet Lake and another steamer that ran to Port Pemberton. From there, a 22-mile wagon road led to Anderson and Seton lakes. Steamers plied those lakes, with a short portage of a mile and a half between, but from the bottom end of Seton Lake, it was only a matter of a few miles into Lillooet. It was a further 47 miles from there to Clinton, which was the junction with the competing route, the Yale and Lytton Wagon Road.

Though an actual road did not exist through the Fraser Canyon until late in 1862, there was a trail that packhorses and mules could manage during the late spring, summer, and early fall months. In fact, it was the one I had come down just four months before in the dead of winter. Tenders had been put out for construction of the road and work was supposed to begin that spring of '62 to improve it, but it would be some time before it was completed.

Even so, the routes were fiercely competitive. The Douglas-Lillooet route was advertised in the *Colonist* as the "Elegant Route to Cariboo." Miners were urged to "Avoid the Lytton Route" because it was "unfinished" and then warned not to be "deceived by the representations of interested parties who will give you all sorts of false information regarding the Lytton Route, and the various distances, which have never yet been measured." On the same page, those working the Lytton Route bragged that it was indeed shorter and that any miner who allowed himself to be duped by the "Douglasites" should expect "no sympathy ... if they get broke trying to get goods through that route."[1]

I chose the latter route on which to make my return to Cariboo even though it would mean negotiating that perilous trail through the Fraser and Thompson canyons again. At least it was the devil that I knew. Moreover, the fact that it was supposedly shorter than the other route by 33 miles was no small consideration when my means of transportation were my own two feet and a pair of snowshoes.

At Yale, 45 of us set out on foot together for the creeks. The way was as tough as I expected, especially through the dangerous gorge above Alexandra Bridge where in places a wrong step could mean certain death. There was still much snow and it wasn't long before the group was strung out over a great distance along the trail as it rose and fell beside the river. Once the country began to flatten out above Hat Creek I was able to increase my speed markedly and left my companions even farther behind. Three weeks later I reached Antler Creek, well ahead of the others who straggled in over the next ten days, the tag end of them footsore and chilblained. The snow along the creek lay at least seven feet deep, but the spring thaw was well under way for there was not an icicle to be seen.

I set to work preparing my building for the arrival of the packers. Meanwhile, other merchants and miners arrived and filled the air around Antler with the sounds of industry: the thud of axes on wood, the crashing of trees to the ground, the scraping of saws across logs, and the banging of hammers on nails and dowels. Soon the creek grew murky from dirt washed through sluices and the miners grew content to be back in the hunt. When the pack trains with their loads of merchandise arrived, I began a booming commission business. Even though the freight costs were as high as 75¢ a pound, I could get five dollars for a pound of nails or a pound of butter, and most items easily went for more than double the cost to get them there. Business proved to be so good that by the time the Camerons arrived on Antler Creek, near the end of July, I had cleared $11,000.

It was a fiercely hot day, the sky streaked with mares' tails, when the Camerons pulled in. Sophia looked exhausted from the long trip, and her expectant condition was now quite apparent. She was trying to console her husband who was fit to be tied. He'd got into an argument with the freighter, Alan McDonald, that began just outside Yale and continued all the way up the road to Quesnelle Forks where McDonald became angry enough that he refused to move our goods an inch farther until he was paid in full for his work. Naturally, Cameron did not have that kind of cash on him, so he and the freighter arrived on Antler Creek with only baleful stares for each other. Our supplies were 45 miles back at the Forks and McDonald wanted $1,400, or he would leave them there. I considered that a fair rate and settled the bill, instructing him to take them instead to Richfield on Williams Creek, because good colour had been reported there. Since Antler Creek appeared to be petering out, that's where I was headed. I sold my business, including the building, for a modest profit and, with the Camerons, made haste across the mountain.

Word of "colour" was a clarion call to miners everywhere, many of whom went dashing off immediately upon hearing the smallest bit of news, without ever verifying it. Some of the more cunning miners, though, would send out fake reports of good prospects on non-gold-bearing creeks so that others would rush there to stake claims, leaving the paying creek to the discoverers. But there was nothing remotely fake about Williams Creek. It would prove to be one of the richest creeks of all time and for a few, the Eldorado they sought.

The creek was named after William Dietz, or "Dutch Bill" as his friends called him. (Bill was actually Prussian, the sobriquet "Dutch" probably being a corruption of "Deutsche.") There are many different versions of Dutch Bill's story, but the one I heard is that, like so many others, he was barely making wages on the lower Fraser River when he heard the reports out of Cariboo. He reached Antler Creek in '61, but by then there wasn't an inch of it left for staking. Since he wasn't about to turn back, he thought there must be other creeks around and set off to investigate the area. He followed Antler to its origins, then climbed above it to a flattop mountain covered by an alpine meadow. Crossing to the far side, he saw another creek off in the distance, descending through a small valley. He followed the rushing water down to where it cut through a small canyon, which looked to be as good a place as any to try his luck. He panned some deposits and found enough colour to warrant staking a claim.

That was in late February of '62. When May rolled around a man named Ned Stout, who was Dutch Bill's partner, was taking out $1,000 a day from his claim. Now some say Ned and Dutch Bill were competitors rather than partners, and that Ned wasn't with Bill when he discovered Williams Creek. Others say there would have been too much snow in February and the discovery wasn't made till May. Such details I leave to the historians to decide upon, but I can say this about Ned Stout: he was one of the most adventurous men I ever knew in

Edward "Ned" Stout, some 50 years after Stevenson met him. He died in 1924 at the ripe old age of 99, proud that he never let tobacco smoke or liquor pass his lips. He is buried in the Pioneer Cemetery at Yale.
(Courtesy of BC Archives G-07958)

Cariboo, and one of the few men who, in later years, would shoot Hell's Gate on a regular basis.

Born in Germany, Ned eventually made his way to North America and the gold creeks of California. He'd made enough money there that when he heard of gold being discovered on the Fraser River, he and a few friends were able to hire a schooner to take them from San Francisco to Bellingham. There they built two scows, which they rowed and sailed all the way to Fort Yale. They worked their way up the Fraser River and onto the Thompson without any trouble, but at the Nicomen Creek confluence they became involved in a fight with the local Indians who were none too happy about white men encroaching on their territory.

Stout and 20 or more other miners beat a hasty retreat and fought a running battle with the Indians back down the Thompson and the Fraser. Men were lost to poisoned arrows along the way, particularly at Jackass Mountain were they were ambushed while crossing an open, rock-slide area. The handful of survivors finally reached China Bar, about 20 miles above Yale, where they built a small fortification. They were under siege for an entire day and night, and two more men were lost. They'd just about reached the end of their luck when a large party of miners from Yale arrived to stave off the attackers. Ned had been hit seven times by arrows. He only survived because the Indians had run out of the rattlesnake poison in which they usually dipped the tips of their arrows.

There had been other skirmishes between the Indians and the miners. One miner, who kept a journal, wrote: "In 1859 I was washing gravel with a rocker 20 miles above Yale. There was some fine gold but not a lot of it. This day I heard the report of a gun and saw a bullet hole in my rocker. I looked around to see where the noise came from and saw an Indian standing on a big rock across the river loading his musket. There was no place I could hide because I was out on a bar and my gun was up on the bank and I was very frightened as I thought I would be shot at any moment. Then I heard another shot and the Indian disappeared off the rock and into the swift water of the Fraser River. I had been very lucky, there was a party of white men working on the same side as the Indian and when they heard him shoot they watched and saw him aim his gun at me and they shot him before he could pull the trigger again. I left that bar that same day and I never mined alone on the Fraser River after that as it was very dangerous since the Indians were not friendly to white men."[2]

The natives were not without some justification for their actions. The same miner wrote: "John Mclean had an experience with Indians in 1860 that was something like mine. Their camp was on the bank of the Fraser a short distance below Soda Creek. He said, 'We made our fire and boiled a big pot of beans and when we were about ready to eat half a dozen Indians came to our camp and wanted some of the beans but we didn't give them any. When they were leaving one of them lifted the lid off the pot and spit on the beans. They knew that the white men would not eat the beans, and after the white men left the camp the Indians would come back and get the beans. After the Indian had spit in the beans the whole party ran for the river. When the spitter was at the edge of the steep slope of the river bank, a young fellow in the white men's party shot him in the back. He jumped high in the air and rolled down the bank into the swift current of the river.'

"The party was very angry at the young man who did the shooting, not because they were in sympathy with the man who spit in their beans, but because their own safety was at stake .... Mr. McLean realized the situation was very serious and says they did not turn in, but hid in the woods all night. He said if we had built our fire and sat around it as we did at other times the chances would be that we would be found by somebody — all dead — shot by the braves."[3]

Governor James Douglas himself came to put an end to the hostilities. He spoke with the Indian chief and insisted that he and his tribe keep the peace, then for added insurance gave him a government sinecure. He told the miners that he would not tolerate any abuses and that the law protecting white men gave equal protection to Indians.

Stout eventually reached Williams Creek and was the first to stake a claim on a dried-up stream bed off Williams, now known as Stout's Gulch. Old Ned is still alive, although I reckon he must be near 90 years old. He lives in Yale and still bends ears with his tales of the Indian Wars and Cariboo.

Compared to Ned Stout, Dutch Bill Dietz didn't have much luck at all. I can't say if it was any consolation to Bill, but they at least named the creek after him. Anyway, we owe them both a vote of thanks because it was mainly their prospects that sent others rushing pell-mell over the mountain from Antler Creek, making a few people rich into the bargain. And I was fortunate enough to count myself among those lucky few.

When I arrived at Williams Creek, it was a storm of human activity in the middle of an indifferent wilderness. Stumbling upon it accidentally would have been very much like a ship running into a fierce squall in the middle of the doldrums.

Several thousand men worked along a mile or so of creek and only a close look would show the order that was in it. The creek itself was no longer recognizable as a creek, diverted as it was in so many places by ditches, channels, wing dams, and wooden flumes with rickety supports. The forest on the surrounding hillsides had been reduced to stumps, yet most of the trees were still there, resurrected as houses, stores, restaurants, hotels, saloons, grog shops, sidewalks, sluices and flumes.

The collection of all those things was called "Richfield." Though it was a small town, it was not like other small towns. Richfield was a place where background and breeding disappeared in the muck and grime of mining, and the new standard of measuring a man's rank in the social order was gold. It was a place where time was a miser that never gave a miner anywhere

Richfield, 1865. (Courtesy of BC Archives G-00795)

near the amount he needed, as days turned rapidly into weeks, weeks into months, and months, all too swiftly, into the end of a mining season. It was a place where a man saw gold in everything around him, where the merest glint off the most irrelevant object made his heart thud in his chest because, for a split second, he believed it was pay dirt. It was a place where the luck of the draw reigned king, where one shaft could be sunk deep into the earth and produce nothing but empty pokes while another, only a few yards away, could give up untold wealth. But most of all, it was a place of unbridled optimism, where the back-breaking toil of today was made tolerable by the promise of tomorrow.

Then, in the wink of an eye, another town sprang up from the wilderness, about a half-mile downstream from Richfield. It was called "Middletown," but would later be renamed Barkerville. And as the gold discoveries moved down the creek, so too did the building and commerce.

Contrary to popular myth, these places were not male sanctuaries. One of the most persistent myths of Cariboo is that there were no women on Williams Creek in those early days. I say without hesitation that nothing could be further from the truth. There were a number of them, mostly wives, including Sophia Cameron. Then there were the prostitutes. My God, but those women were a vile lot. Most of them dressed like men and emulated our worst habits of cursing, smoking, chewing tobacco, spitting, and drinking more whiskey than any decent person ought to. But men need women and that is the way of the world, so their presence was tolerated. Most of the miners, myself included, were grateful when the more conventional saloons and bawdy houses displaced them. (Lest

Chapter Five

I be accused of exaggerating the offensiveness of these women, I offer substantiation from the *Colonist* dated September 10, 1862, when it was reported that there were nine prostitutes on Williams Creek who "put on great airs. They dress in male attire and swagger through the saloons and mining camps with cigars and huge qwids [*sic*] of tobacco in their mouths, cursing and swearing and look like anything but the angels in petti-coats heaven intended them to be. Each has a revolver or bowie knife attached to her waist, and it is quite a common occurrence to see one or more women dressed in male attire playing poker in the saloons, or drinking whiskey at the bars. They are a degraded set, and all good men in the vicinity wish them hundreds of miles away.")

The other great myth that needs dispelling is that those min-ing towns were lawless places where men and women did as they pleased with impunity. That also is a long way from the truth. On Williams Creek, it was always best to think twice before pursuing any nefarious pastimes. Miners who stepped outside the law, whether it was something as simple as being drunk and disorderly or the graver crime of brandishing a knife or gun, stood a reasonably good chance of meeting the likes of Matthew Baillie Begbie.

Judge Begbie was not a man to tangle with either physically or mentally. He was big and strong, and thought better on his feet than any man I've ever encountered. No stranger to the lib-eral arts, he was also strict and represented law and order in its most authoritative, paternalistic form. In some ways he could be likened to the American cowboy who shot first and asked questions later, except that Begbie asserted law and order first and then worried about whether it was within his jurisdiction

During his first dozen years as a judge, Matthew Baillie Begbie, centre, sentenced more than two dozen men to the gallows. After his death, he became known as "The Hanging Judge." The imposing size of the man, even sitting down, can be seen in this photograph. (COURTESY OF BC ARCHIVES A-01102)

to do so. And there was no one around Cariboo bold enough to question him on it.

He was a fair man, though, and meted out justice equally to all who came before him, regardless of creed or colour. He was never shy about issuing punishments that would fit the crime, to ensure there'd be no repeat offenders. And many a jury experienced his wrath when he thought their verdict was wrong. In one case, a man had been sandbagged, or clubbed over the head, and left to die in the street. Much to Begbie's amazement, the jury acquitted the man charged with the crime. The judge turned to the accused and said, "Prisoner at the bar, the jury have said you are not guilty. You can go, and I devoutly hope the next man you sandbag will be one of the jury!"[4]

I believe it was because of men like him that violence and bloodshed in those gold towns never got out of hand as they did in California and Nevada. As one miner put it, Begbie was "the damnedest man that ever came over the Cariboo Road."[5]

Usually, though, Begbie and his colleagues were saved a lot of work simply because the miners didn't have time to get into trouble. If I were allowed only three words to describe that town and the creek, the first would be "busy" and the other two would be synonyms of that word. Of the 8,000 miners who were on Williams Creek that season, there were few idle hands, since sitting around was not an affordable luxury. Everyone worked hard, probably harder than they'd ever done in their lives.

Not only did it take a major effort with considerable risk just to get to the goldfields, there was backbreaking work waiting for the miner once he arrived. First, he needed a place to live — a tent was good only temporarily — which meant building a cabin. Trees had to be felled, notched, fitted together and chinked. Then a roof had to be put on, usually of shakes that were hand split. Once that was done and he was ready to dig for gold, something was needed to wash the dirt, such as a rocker, a Long Tom, or a sluice. Or maybe he needed a flume to bring water to his claim, (one flume was four miles long!) or perhaps a water wheel to pump water out of it.

Any serious search for gold required either deep shafts sunk to the bedrock, or long tunnels dug into a hillside, both of which could easily cave in if they weren't braced properly. To prevent that from happening they were lined with timbers, all of which meant that more trees needed falling. The bigger ones had to be either split with an axe or ripped with a whipsaw if there was one available. (Whipsawing required two men and a pit deep enough for one of them to stand in. The log to be ripped into lumber was laid over the hole, and one man stood above the log while the other stood below. Together they worked the long saw up and down, up and down, until they hoped their arms would fall off before their hearts stopped. The man in the pit ate sawdust while flies and mosquitoes ate the man above.[6]) Nails to join two pieces of wood together were expensive and often scarce so the miners whittled dowels by hand and then banged them into holes drilled with a hand auger.

For many, the toil continued long into the night, when the darkness was pierced by pinholes of light from lanterns marking the mine entrances, and a pall of wood smoke hung over the valley. The constant din of the busyness that filled the daytime — the hammering, the sawing, and the constant groaning of water wheels — only lessened when night fell, without ever quite disappearing.

It's my belief that idle men usually stayed home and never flirted with a mistress as demanding as a mining claim. The men I knew were the hardest workers God ever put on this earth. And if mining didn't cripple or maim them, it sometimes sent them to an early grave.

Yet a miner needed more than a penchant for hard work if he hoped to be successful. The greenhorns worked as hard as anyone, but they depended too much on Lady Luck being a silent partner. It certainly helped to have her on your side, but the most successful miners were the experienced ones who understood the biography of gold and the best ways to retrieve it.

When gold is in its molten form, it finds its way into cracks in the surrounding rock. Those gold-filled cracks are called "veins" or "lodes." Over long periods of time they are subject to tremendous natural forces that break them down into flakes or nuggets that are eventually washed downhill into streams and rivers by rain or melting snow. These in turn collect on sand and gravel bars along the course of the waterway, and are called "placer" (the "a" here is pronounced like the "a" in "plan") deposits. There are different kinds of placers, but the Cariboo miner was generally concerned with the one laid down by a stream, called a "stream placer." Sometimes these deposits could be found near the surface and retrieved with a simple gold pan. However, since gold is extremely heavy, in time it will usually work its way down through the stream bed to the bedrock. That kind of gold has to be excavated.

Excavations were generally in the form of tunnels or pits, sometimes a combination of the two. Tunnels were dug horizontally into hillsides and followed gold seams, often for long distances underground. This was called "drift" mining. More typical, though, were pits, which were dug vertically until gold was reached, at which point the miners would drift horizontally along the seam. At the top of the pit was a windlass that was used to bring up barrels of dirt. This was simply a drum with a rope and bucket dangling from it that could be cranked up and down, just like getting water from a well. What came up was rarely pure gold but earth that had to be washed to determine whether or not it was gold-bearing. There were several ways of doing this.

The most basic was the simple gold pan, a versatile tool that could also be used for cooking. It required more skill to use than most people thought, but basically, a pan was filled with sand and gravel and some water from a stream or a flume. This mixture was then worked, or kneaded, with the hands to get rid of the larger rocks. After that, the pan was shaken back and forth, which allowed the heavier gold to sink to the bottom. Then it was just a matter of rotating the pan while it was slightly submerged in the water to allow the finer material to sift out. On a good day, what was left in the pan might put a miner one step closer to being a wealthy man, or at least cover his expenses and pay him a decent wage.

There was also a "dry washing" method that consisted of pulverizing gravel with a mortar, then flipping it up and down on a flat sheet so that the wind blew away the finer material. It was a cumbersome way of looking for gold and was only used when wet washing wasn't available.

Both panning and dry washing were pretty slow ways to separate gold from placer deposits, but they were cheap and a good way to tell if the ground being worked contained gold. Once that was determined, it was time to move into full operation by building a rocker, a Long Tom or a sluice box. All of these operated on the same principle; that is, they were designed to use water to wash the dirt along, with a series of riffles or cleats on the bottom to trap the gold as it sank. The major difference was their size.

A rocker was simply a box, about five feet long, with one end open and a hopper at the other. The hopper was filled with dirt and water, then the box was rocked back and forth. Larger material stayed behind in the hopper while smaller material — gravel, sand, and gold — was washed through to the riffled bottom. The lighter sand and gravel washed over the cleats while the heavier gold was caught by them. A Long Tom, on the other hand, might have been up to three times the length of a rocker and was fixed flat on the ground with a constant supply of water running through it. Dirt was shovelled into it and water did most of the rest of the work, just like in the rocker. A sluice box was merely a raised and longer version of a Long Tom, and in most cases was connected to a flume. Naturally, more dirt could be washed in the larger devices. But a Long Tom and sluice box required more than one man to keep them productive and that was one of the reasons why miners formed companies. The more men there were, the more dirt could be processed with, they hoped, greater dividends.

Water was the key to it all, though, as necessary to the process as blood is to life. If there wasn't a source in the immediate vicinity then it had to be brought in, hence the construction of flumes and water wheels.

When our freight finally arrived on Williams Creek, Cameron noticed that a few items had gone missing, namely some flour and butter. Other pack trains had similar complaints but all we could do was report it to Judge Begbie when he came around. The missing provisions may have gone astray at Quesnelle Forks, but it is also likely that they were stolen at 24 Mile House on the Port Douglas-Pemberton road. In August of 1862, the proprietor of the house, James Joice, and his partner, were caught red-handed stealing goods from freight wagons passing through and were subsequently arrested. Apparently, they'd been doing it for some time.

I was relieved to see that among the supplies that did arrive, there were several cases of candles. They were in 20-pound boxes and in extremely poor condition, most having been broken in the jouncing around they received on the backs of the pack animals. Nevertheless, candles were scarce in Cariboo and those cases represented a small fortune. I went from claim to claim and with no trouble at all sold every last one of them for $100 per box. We'd paid only a few dollars for them back in Victoria, but the miners were more than willing to pay practically any price we named.

Lest it be thought that I was taking advantage of the miners, let me say that I was only taking advantage of a good business opportunity. The law of supply and demand was in full swing up and down the creek, and some astute merchants were making small fortunes.

I remember two in particular, not because of how well they did with their business, but because of what happened to them and a packer the day after the Camerons arrived in Antler. It caused a great stir on the creeks where it was known as the "murder of the Jews." I believe the names of the merchants were Sokoloski and Lewin, but I can't recall the packer's name.

They left Antler for the coast with about $11,000 in gold dust between them. Near where the trail between Keithley Creek and Quesnelle Forks crosses the Cariboo River, bandits waylaid them. They must have put up a fierce fight to save themselves, since all their guns were empty of bullets. All three had been shot through the head and Sokoloski had also been viciously beaten. The men who did it were never found, but everyone believed that one of them was that Oregon madman, Boone Helm.

Helm was a nasty customer who may have been certifiably insane. He was also a cannibal, having eaten his partner while they were snowbound in a mountain pass, and God knows the number of people he murdered. But I don't think he murdered the Jews, because some things don't jibe. Grave markers in the Quesnelle Forks cemetery record their deaths as being on July 26, 1862. But the *Colonist* and court records bear witness to the fact that Helm was in Victoria during October, being held in jail for a month because of his inability to pay a fine assessed against him for causing trouble in the Adelphi Saloon. If he had committed the murders, then he must have just recently come down from Cariboo; if that were the case, surely the authorities would have known by then that he was suspected of the killings and held him pending an investigation. Instead, he was unleashed on the world again. I understand that he eventually got what was coming to him and was hanged for horse stealing in Virginia City in 1864.

While making the rounds selling candles, I met a Doc Crane — he wasn't a medical doctor, the title was only a nickname — who told me about an unclaimed stretch along Williams Creek and said that if I wanted it I'd better get over there as quickly as possible to stake it. I immediately set up a company that included the Camerons, Alan McDonald, Dick Rivers, Charles and James Clendenning and myself. Initially, Doc Crane was a partner, but he forfeited that right after shooting at a man in a Richfield saloon, for which the local judge gave him 30 days in jail. We didn't want such a man in our company.

Besides, during the winter, Crane had been accused of stealing some gin from a store in Victoria. I recalled reading about that episode in the *Colonist*; when he returned to the very same store and the proprietor tried to evict him, Crane pulled a knife and attempted to stab the man. He spent the night in jail and was released only because the proprietor declined to prosecute. Crane said he'd defy any man to prove he'd stolen the gin, so I was willing to give him the benefit of the doubt, but the shooting proved that he was trouble looking for a place to happen and therefore not a man with whom we ought to associate.

Everything was in place and all that was left to do was stake the claim. But, unbelievably, Cameron refused. It was Friday, he pointed out, and Fridays were unlucky. He would not make a move till Saturday.

I must be frank here and say that Cameron's superstition tried my patience considerably. I could understand his altercation with McDonald, because both were obstinate men, but in this case, time was surely of the essence. If we didn't move quickly, it might be that we would be unable to move at all. Yet, something held me back from asserting my position in the matter. Maybe it was those eyes that seemed to look right through a person. Or perhaps I was simply obeying a surrogate father. To this day, I'm at a loss to fully explain my behaviour around Cameron, but whatever the reasons were, I acquiesced. Saturday it was.

When we reached the spot, Cameron and I argued over where we should stake the claim. I wanted to stake on the right bank, which is the bank to the right when one is facing downstream, but he insisted that we stake on the left. I had reservations about his suggestion, but bowed to his greater placer experience. As it turned out, the right bank was rich with gold. Indeed, Henry Beatty, one of the owners of that claim, eventually became a charter member of the syndicate that built the Canadian Pacific Railroad. Nevertheless, on Monday, August 25, in the Year of Our Lord 1862, we officially registered our claim. Since Cameron chose the spot, we named it after him.[7]

We could barely contain our excitement because on that "unlucky" Friday Cameron was so concerned about, less than a half-mile up the creek, a man named Barker was making history.

William Barker, or Billy, as we called him, was a short man with an even shorter temper, and a thick, straggly beard. He had more histories than any man I ever knew, and the version you got depended on whom you talked to. A popular one is that he was a British naval seaman who jumped ship in Victoria. All the way up the coast from California, he'd heard reports of gold in Cariboo, and when he reached Victoria he knew it was time to become a drylander again. His trademark was a big-buckled sailor's belt that he always wore, just in case the Royal Navy found him. Back in those days they hanged deserters but were relatively lenient with people who were merely absent without leave. The way a man could prove he was not a deserter was to show as evidence something that obviously connected him to the navy; it supposedly indicated an intention to return. So Billy kept his belt and always wore it. When he began looking for gold on Williams Creek the other miners laughed at him. They thought he was looking in the wrong place, but Barker outsmarted them all.

That's the Billy Barker story heard most often, but I always thought there was more to him than that. For a common seaman, he had an uncanny sense of how gold behaves over the ages. I never believed for a moment that was intuition, and I think that he was no more a seaman than I am capable of flying one of those strange contraptions that have been leaving the ground like ungainly birds for the past few years. I'd wager my last poke of gold that he more than likely cut his teeth on the creeks of California for many years before he arrived in Cariboo, maybe even during the early rush to the Fraser River as well. That irascible old coot knew a whole lot more about mining gold than he ever let on.

However he came upon the knowledge, Billy accurately reasoned that if gold could be found in a wet stream bed, then it might also be found in a dry one. When he arrived at the creek he went downstream from most of the activity and saw a likely place where the creek had probably been diverted hundreds of years before. That's where he started digging. And that's when people started laughing. He dug down 10, 20, 30, all the way to 40 feet and found nothing. The miners looked at each other knowingly.

But Barker wasn't about to give up. He'd had recurring dreams in which the words "pay at 52" were repeated over and over, and he was sure he knew what that meant. He kept on digging. From dusk till dawn there was a man in the pit, shovelling dirt into an oak barrel that other men hauled up on the windlass. Still others washed it. At 52 feet, he found nothing. Nor did he find anything at 53 or 54 feet and he was beginning to think that perhaps his critics were right, that maybe he really was on the wild goose chase of his life. But if he was anything, Billy was a persistent man so he kept at it.

At 55 feet he hit pay dirt. Every pan yielded five dollars in gold — a lot of money when a labourer on the creeks then made only four dollars a day. He kept on digging, and at 80 feet reached bedrock and found even more gold. He'd struck it rich and miners were scrambling to stake claims down the length of the creek, especially where wet and dry gulches led into it. Williams Creek had turned from something merely promising into a full-blown bonanza.[8]

Our claim was also located where a small stream entered Williams Creek but downstream from Barker's. The day that we staked it was only three days after Billy Barker struck it rich, so we moiled away what was left of the summer, encouraged by Barker's uncanny luck and fired by a robust optimism. But summer soon turned into the shortest fall I'd ever reckoned with and a heavy snowfall blanketed us by late September. The miners began disappearing in droves, heading down to Victoria for the winter, until there was only a smattering of us left.

We'd sunk a shaft that reached bedrock but found nothing. That completely demoralized the Clendennings who refused to

Billy Barker, second from the left, at the windlass of his Williams Creek claim.
(COURTESY OF BC ARCHIVES A-03858)

work any more and left for Victoria themselves. They also refused to leave behind any money to help start a new shaft, which was a hardship because our expenses had been as high as $7,000 for a single week. We started one anyway, but each day that we toiled and came away empty-handed not only chipped away at our pocketbooks, it also eroded our pride and optimism. And to make matters worse, typhoid, or "mountain fever" as we called it, found Williams Creek to be a pretty good place to stake a claim too. We'd dug holes in the ground for toilets and when it rained or flooded, the waste seeped into our drinking water and poisoned some of us with that awful disease. We had no idea what we were doing to ourselves.

Chapter Six

WHILE WE WERE caught up in our search for gold, Sophia Cameron was having a devil of a time. Not long after her arrival on the creeks she went into labour prematurely and gave birth to a stillborn baby. Since there was no cemetery yet on Williams Creek, the baby was wrapped in a cloth, taken up the hillside, and buried in a shallow grave that was covered with rocks to keep the animals away.

The Camerons, who were not fully recovered from Mary's death, were shattered by this turn of events. They had hoped the baby would help fill the void caused by losing Mary but instead, it had only grown deeper and wider. Cameron's sorrow was laden with guilt, as he felt solely responsible for their misfortunes. Had he not insisted that Sophia accompany him here, these tragedies would most certainly not have occurred. Nevertheless, they had come too far, their investment too great, to even consider for a moment turning back. The stubborn streak he possessed was never more evident than in his determination to carry on. As for Sophia, it was simply more pain added to an already painful situation.

It might have been tolerable had she not hated Cariboo so intensely. But the mountains penned her in like walls of a prison, and when dark, heavy clouds slid down the ravaged slopes to fill the valley, as they did far too frequently for her liking, she thought she might suffocate. She longed for the broad sweep of the skies above Glengarry and Cornwall, the farms, and the great river that rolled by. Most of all, she longed for her family — so much her very soul ached. Yet, through all her suffering, I never once heard her complain. Indeed, she pitched in wherever she could, and though her heart was not in it, she seemed to have more energy than the rest of us put together. She was usually first up in the morning and the last in bed at night, filling her day with preparing meals — often for me and others as well — cleaning up, fetching water from the creek, and doing laundry for almost any man on our claim who asked. The displeasure she felt for her circumstances was only apparent periodically, in the taught muscles of a clenched jaw or an uncharacteristic terseness. Cameron was sensitive to these moods and went out of his way to be gentle with her. Though he was not an overtly affectionate man, his eyes, which usually could not be read, always held her in adoration.

My admiration for Sophia increased daily. She deserved something far better than a mining camp and thankless menial chores, yet she conducted herself with grace in the face of these adversities. Then one day, out of the blue, she voiced her first complaint. She said that she had a terrible headache and was feeling quite feverish. She took to her bed earlier than usual that evening and when she was not at her chores first thing in the morning, and was gasping from abdominal pain, we knew it was mountain fever.

Luckily, there was a doctor in Richfield. Cameron called on Dr. Wilkinson, who visited Sophia and performed the rituals known only to men of that profession. He prescribed some medicine for her and gave us directions as to how and when to administer it. From that point on, Cameron spent many of his waking hours tending to his wife's needs. It was such a demanding task that some of the women who remained behind that winter also helped. The two whose names I recall were Anna Cameron, who was not related to John, and Scotch Jenny, who was a Barkerville fixture and who might have taught Florence Nightingale a thing or two about charity. She was one of those people who are indispensable in small communities and was always helping others whenever she could. She was especially generous with her time when it came to nursing sick people. The poor woman was killed one night in 1870, while she was driving her buggy home. It went over an embankment and she suffered a broken neck.[1]

I, especially, felt obliged to spell Cameron off from his duties. We set up an irregular schedule and took turns so that someone was with Sophia day and night. When it came my turn, I would leave from either the cabin that I shared with two other miners near the diggings, or the claim itself if I was working, and make my way up the creek to the Cameron cabin in Richfield. During that period the weather turned so brutally cold that the air felt brittle and the snow crunched under my feet like gravel. Yet never for an instant did I feel that I wasn't involved in the best of causes. I was inordinately fond of Sophia and cared for her as if she were my own.

One night as Cameron was relieving me, she had one of her brief lucid moments and pleaded with him that if she died, he must promise not to leave her in that Godforsaken place. "It is not death I'm afraid of," she said hoarsely, the words nearly lost among the eerie sounds emitted by the cabin's logs as they contracted in the frigid weather. "My only fear is of spending eternity here among these wretched mountains. I know that what I ask may seem impossible, but I beg of you, John, please take me home."

Her gaunt face seemed more grey than bronze now, and beads of sweat formed on her forehead. The desperation in her voice was such that Cameron did not hesitate. He reached for her hand and clasped it between both of his. "I will do it," he said, his voice cracking. "If it's my last earthly act, I will do it. As God is my witness, I will take you home. You have my word on it."

How Cameron was able to contain himself, I cannot say, but I believe that if there were a power that would have allowed him to exchange places with her, he would not have delayed a moment in calling upon it. I could see a slight trembling in his shoulders as he reached for a cloth, and also in the hand that began to wipe Sophia's brow. There was such tenderness and love in his touch that I had to turn away, for fear that I myself might crumble.

Throughout the last days of Sophia's life, Cameron and I did everything within our power to alleviate her suffering and make her well again. There were times when she rallied and we thought she might get better, when she fought her affliction with the great strength she possessed and seemed to beat it back, but it was merely a skirmish won in a battle she would ultimately lose. It was as if she were climbing a great mountain and could get only so far before it defeated her. Each day the mountain got a little higher, the climb a little steeper and the slide down a little farther into that place where the thought of having to climb back up again becomes unbearable and death is an acceptable alternative. Her fever soared and she was plagued by a persistent dry cough, sometimes so severe that it wracked her wasting body. When the will to live began to wane in those beautiful dark eyes, it was heartwrenching. We prayed for her and we prayed for us, that we would not lose her, but our prayers went unanswered.

On the night Sophia died the wind howled up Williams Creek like a wolf gone mad, a fitting end to a day that had begun dull and grey, the harbinger of a storm that by noon had bullied its way up the valley with stinging pellets of ice and roiling clouds that hid the snow-draped mountains. The thermometer stood at 30 below zero, cold enough even without the fierce wind.

I had gone to their cabin about midnight, tramping through the deep snow, to relieve Cameron. It was cold inside, despite the wood fire we always kept blazing. That mattered little to Sophia, though; she was herself on fire. Soon after I arrived, her fever began to subside and her skin grew as pale as if her blood were leaking from her body. I felt her pulse and it was weak and slow. By three o'clock in the morning, her face had taken on a peaceful cast and her breathing grew shallow, so I awoke Cameron to say she was slipping away and that he should prepare himself for her departure. There was nothing more we could do.

He sat on the edge of the bed, a simple pallet on a platform, and took her hands in his. "They are so cold," he whispered to no one in particular, and in that instant, it seemed, life left her. He laid his head on her breast, grief spilling from his eyes, as if the entire world had been lost to him, which, in a sense, I suppose it had. I gave him time to collect himself — indeed, I needed some time myself — then gripped his shoulders and led him away from his dead wife. I pulled the blanket up over her still-beautiful face, composed and serene now in death, and glanced over at Cameron. The hurt and despair that I had seen on his face that early March morning in Victoria when Mary died had returned, lodged there so firmly I thought it might never leave again.

By daybreak, the storm had blown itself out. A thin band of light was slowly widening above the eastern ridges as I sought out a tinsmith and a carpenter. If Cameron was indeed going to return Sophia's remains to her childhood home, a specially adapted coffin would be needed. I called on Jim Griffin, a skilled carpenter, and Henry Lightfoot, an equally adept tinsmith, and had them make two coffins, one from tin that would fit inside another made from wood. There was no undertaker in Richfield to attend to Sophia, so Griffin and I placed her in the metal casket ourselves. I folded a beautiful knitted shawl, one that was a gift from her mother, and placed it under her head as a pillow, then stuffed some old clothing around her so that she would not be battered on the rough trip that awaited her. Lightfoot sealed the tin case shut and Griffin nailed the wooden lid on top.

The funeral service was held in the small chapel in Richfield and of the 90 miners and the handful of women who had stayed in camp that winter, all attended. There wasn't one among them who didn't share at least some of Cameron's grief, and all hoped that Sophia's passing had taken her to a better place than the one from which she had departed much too soon. Afterward, her remains were placed in an empty, unheated cabin where the sub-zero temperatures would preserve her until it came time to move her to the coast. It was a long and difficult road she'd travelled to reach this far-off place, but she would soon be going home. Cameron had promised her, and he'd proven to be a man of his word.

We went back to work. It not only seemed the best thing to do — there was nothing else we *could* do. Cameron worked feverishly, for each idle moment only served to remind him of his tremendous losses. I knew his sorrow and kept pace with him, pushing myself to the outer limits of my abilities and energy until it seemed exhaustion was all I'd ever known. In those spiritually low moments, I despaired that we'd ever find anything.

One night, after leaving the pit for my cabin, I was certain that I'd had enough placering in that north country to last a lifetime. I felt more cold and miserable than I had ever thought possible and longed to be home. A cancer of despair had begun eating away at the very core of my optimism and upon retiring, I sensed a change deep within me, a change I once believed could never happen.

For the first time since I'd left Glengarry, I had doubts about my presence on those creeks, a thought that perhaps my life thus far had been a colossal waste of time. A much wiser person, I told myself, would have tried to make his fortune from the miners instead of from mining. As it was, most of the money I'd made was gone, invested in what was beginning to look more and more like a worthless piece of ground. I thought about my family, my father in particular, and the bragging assurance I had given him what seemed like eons ago. I couldn't go back empty-handed. Not that he would care. I was his son and he'd know that I had tried my best. So would I, but it would always hurt to know that I hadn't quite measured up.

I was so full of self-doubt and self-pity that I tossed and turned for hours before I finally fell asleep. I don't know when I've felt more miserable. Come morning, my perspective wasn't showing a lot of improvement, but the way things turned out I might have put my thoughts to a more constructive use.

Monday, December 22, dawned clear, with the air so cold it could scarcely be breathed. After breakfast, I met Dick Rivers and a hired hand named Bill Halpenny at the digging, and we set ourselves to another long day's toil. The previous day Rivers and I had taken a new shaft down to 14 feet when we encountered water, so Halpenny was hired to help clean it up. We hauled up several barrels of water before the bottom was reasonably dry, then shored the walls. After that, we got down to 22 feet, with Rivers at the bottom of the shaft filling the barrels with earth while Halpenny and I operated the windlass. Cameron, who was working another shaft on the claim, had just arrived on the scene when Dick hollered up, with great excitement in his voice, that we should get down there at once. "The place," he exclaimed, "is yellow with gold! Look here, boys!"

I lay down on the platform and peered into the depths just as Rivers held up a flat rock the size of a dinner plate. Even in the candlelight, the gold protruding from it was as plain as ears on a mule. Rivers, big drops of sweat glistening on his forehead, put it in the barrel and we hauled it up. There turned out to be $16 worth of gold in that rock. Cameron hurried down the ladder into the shaft while I grabbed my pick and poked through some of the now-frozen gravel we'd brought up earlier. My heart was pounding in my chest. I quickly found another $16, and by the time I'd worked through the rest of it, about three 12-gallon barrels full, I'd found $155 more. When Cameron came back up, he was nearly breathless with excitement.

"We've done it, Stevenson! We've hit pay dirt, and even if the streak doesn't go beyond what I can see of it, we'll be rich men!"

We gripped each other by the arms, and swung about in a half-circle that from a distance must have looked like a strange dance, which I suppose it was — the dance of two men who dreamed a dream and lived it. Or perhaps it was the dance of two men who didn't quite know the right steps, for Cameron's eyes spoke of what I felt: that while we had achieved something great, it would always be incomplete without the one person we needed to share it with the most.

Once the euphoria of the moment passed, our first reaction was to withhold the news of our discovery from everyone else on the creek, but after weighing the idea, we realized that it was next to impossible to keep such secrets in a mining camp. We let everyone know that Christmas had come three days early to the owners of the Cameron claim. There were grins as wide as the valley and backs were slapped hard enough to knock an unsuspecting man down. Then we seriously depleted a keg of the finest Hudson's Bay rum.

Over the ensuing days we sank the shaft all the way down to bedrock at 38 feet and found gold every inch of the way. Williams Creek had just yielded what would ultimately prove to be its richest pay streak ever. And as we worked the days away, a question weighed as heavy as gold on our hearts: how might things have turned out had this discovery been made sooner? The answer was too painful to contemplate.

Cameron was anxious to get Sophia's remains to the coast. Not only could he afford it now, but he needed to beat the spring thaw so that she would stay preserved. He put out an offer in the camp, stating that he would pay any man $12 a day, with a bonus of $2,000, for help in transporting the coffin. He reasoned that for those miners who were digging and not finding anything, it would be a good way to earn some expense money. It may well have been, but no one took him up on his offer. Smallpox lay in ambush all the way to Victoria and the miners feared for their lives.

Cameron came to me in a quandary. He told me of the men's fears, adding that he didn't blame them a bit. Hardly a day went by that we didn't hear of somebody being stricken with that terrible disease, but he was clearly disappointed with his fellow miners. I immediately offered my services, even though we had originally agreed that I would stay behind and look after the claim. He refused, protesting, "You have never had the smallpox and I would not forgive myself if you caught it."

"That's a risk I'm more than willing to take," I said, and when he objected on the grounds that we needed someone to run the claim, I suggested a mutual friend we both trusted. Cameron hesitated, mulling the idea over for a moment.

Then he locked his eyes on mine and sighed. "Well, if you will go, Stevenson, I would rather have you than any man in Cariboo."

Without thinking, I blurted, "I'll go, and what's more, I'll go all the way to Glengarry when the time comes. You can keep your money, too. I'll pay my own expenses. But you must promise me one thing. It will not be easy for you to open Sophia's coffin once you get it back home, but you must. Her relatives and friends will expect it. I want your word that you will."

"You have it," he said.

I felt strongly about this because I feared that my friend might falter and not keep the custom of opening the casket, being unable to gaze upon Sophia's face. But I knew that those back home would need a last glimpse of their loved one, and more important, they would need to be reassured that the casket did indeed contain her remains. Therefore I deemed it imperative that Cameron satisfy those needs, regardless of how difficult the task might be.

And why had I made such a bold offer? It came from the deep sympathy I felt for my friend, who had lost a wife and two children in less than eight months, and from a lesson well learned — the one that my father had taught me about helping others. And surely it came from the depth of my feelings toward Sophia herself. Even so, I was no fool and knew the seriousness and the possible consequences of the journey we were about to undertake. So, apparently, did Cameron, for his eyes had grown wide with surprise. Before he had time to voice any further objections, or dissuade me with reason, I hastily added that I had important business to attend to and excused myself. I might easily have changed my mind.

Later, Cameron went up to the Barker claim and brought Billy down to ours. Together they descended into the pit where Cameron showed the diminutive Englishman what we had found. Barker was impressed, for he knew that he'd been outdone. On the strength of what he saw, he loaned Cameron 50 pounds of gold dust until our claim could be worked properly in the spring.

Chapter Seven

WELL BEFORE DAYLIGHT on January 31, 1863, we pulled a sled to the door of the cabin that held Sophia's remains. Our breath puffed out as ice clouds in the still, morning air that felt as fragile as crystal. We had to lean our shoulders into the door because it had frozen shut. It suddenly sprang open and scraped over the rough plank floor with a sound that might have wakened the dead. The coffin sat forlornly in the gloom and Cameron paused beside it, a gloved hand resting on top. I gave him a moment, then together we carried it outside, placed it on the sled and covered it with a canvas tarpaulin before securing it with ropes. Then we eased the awkward load down the short slope to the flat road bisecting the town. From Cameron's cabin we fetched the gold poke, a two-gallon keg of good quality Hudson's Bay rum, several blankets we would need for sleeping, sundry supplies that included an axe and as much grub as we could manage, and lashed it all on the top of the coffin. Lastly, we attached a long lead rope to the front. Altogether, it was a preposterously top-heavy load, for the sled's runners were only 14 inches apart. Yet somehow we had to haul that cumbersome thing several hundred miles through the mountains to the coast.

The first obstacle we faced was right at our front door: a mountain of no small size. Cameron and I could not get that load up there by ourselves, but several of the miners had offered to help us get to the other side, at least as far as Tom Maloney's roadhouse, in a small valley below Bald Mountain. A few others said they would go as far as Beaver Lake, at which point Cameron and I would be on our own. That was where the smallpox was waging war against the Indians.

We all wore snowshoes, for there were two feet of freshly fallen snow on top of six feet of old, compacted snow that had accumulated over the winter. The going was tough the moment we stepped outside the camp, and stretching up before us was the mountain, the lower reaches stripped of trees, the upper thickly forested.

We zigzagged up the steep slope along a switchback trail that was barely visible in the snow, 26 of us in a line, pulling on the long rope attached to the sled. Several times the load tipped over and slid down to the last traverse and we'd have to start again. Finally, we stationed men on the sides and behind and with considerable effort and perseverance, reached the trees where the snow wasn't as deep. As the trail rose along the mountainside it became more difficult to follow, and higher up it petered out altogether. By noon we had managed to cover only a scant three and a half miles and it became evident that if we did not pick up our pace we would be unlikely to reach the safety and shelter of Maloney's roadhouse. The higher we climbed the colder it got, and by the time we crossed a ridge the temperature had fallen to 25 below. The sky — what could be seen of it through the trees — was leaden, and the wind moaned in the branches overhead. Without a trail to follow, or the sun to offer direction, some of the men became disoriented. I had been appointed leader and guide, though, and felt certain I knew where we were. I bore off to the left amongst the dense green timber until we came to a winding, snow-smothered notch that I knew had to be Grouse Creek. Everyone worried that I was leading us deeper into the maze of the forest from which there'd be no escape. We struggled up the creek, pulling our heavy load, and righting it the countless times it tipped over. Night fell and still we continued, while the wind pummelled us and piled the snow up like ocean waves. At last we broke out of the trees into an open, flat area and saw through the blowing snow the flicker of light from the windows of Tom Maloney's house. We arrived exhausted and staggering, our enormous expenditure of energy having brought us a mere eight miles.

We passed the night in comparative luxury, bodies scattered every which way about the floor, albeit as close as possible to the stone fireplaces located at each end of the house. The next morning we awoke to the sound of the wind, still blowing a gale, while the temperature had sunk to 35 below. The entire flat around Maloney's, so exposed to the wind, was piled high with great drifts of snow, and the cabin itself was nearly buried. Fourteen of the miners turned back for Richfield with our profuse thanks. We would not have made it to Maloney's without them. The rest of us struck out through the dry, loose snow to see what further hardship we could inflict upon ourselves.

Our mufflers were wound around our heads so that only our eyes were exposed — anything short of that was to risk certain frostbite. The wind continued to howl, and blew the powdery snow from the drift crests like spindrift on a stormy sea. It was as if some great angry giant was pelting us with sand. Huge gusts lifted even more snow high into the air like smoke, and each man could barely see the back of the man in front.

We fought our way through the drifts, our snowshoes sinking uselessly into them. The snow contained so little moisture that it wouldn't support our weight. With much sweat and strain we soon were away from the open flat and among the trees. The conditions improved ever so slightly, but we still had to deal with that confounded sled, which kept toppling over. Every little slant on our path threatened to upset it and usually did. Then we'd heave it upright again — all 500 pounds of it — and each righting required more energy than the last. We moved at a snail's pace, with prodigious effort, up over a barren, windswept plateau where the world turned so white from blowing snow it was as if the very heavens had descended upon us, though God himself seemed far away. The trees on the far slope were a welcome refuge in which to make camp for the night.

We came upon a great lichen-covered rock with some level ground on its lee side. While I knocked as much snow as I could from the limbs of the trees overhead, so that it wouldn't melt and fall on top of our fire, others gathered wood and cut boughs for mattresses. Using our snowshoes as shovels, we dug our campsite out of the deep snow, building a rampart around the edge for an added windbreak. We got a good fire blazing and set up a watch schedule to keep it that way. Then exhaustion overtook us and we slept, the men nodding off one by one, their snores mixing with the crackling fire. We had only our blankets for protection from the cold, but they were Hudson's Bay blankets of superior quality and we were quite warm next to the fire. That night Cameron hung his spirit thermometer from a nearby tree and in the morning it registered 50 below.

It was the practice of the Indians to cut down saplings along the trails in summer so that they would have seasoned firewood in winter. The miners sometimes duplicated this trick and on another night we found along our path a small stand of toppled trees with which we built long fires. We could then could stretch out on either side and warm the entire length of our bodies. We spent a reasonably comfortable night that way, helped, for a change, by a lack of wind.

The days piled on top of each other as we reached the Swift River and left it behind, turning south over a ridge toward Snowshoe Creek that would eventually lead us to Davis' Crossing on Keithley Creek. As we climbed, the snow lay deeper and every step forward was a battle won. It was along that Godforsaken stretch that our food ran out.

There was little we could do but press on and ignore the nagging hunger pangs. Still, we had one important consolation: the two-gallon keg of rum lashed to the top of the coffin. Its contents wouldn't fill our bellies but they would at least give us the luxury of forgetting our hunger, if only for a brief time.

We were working our way along the rim of a steep embankment when the sled toppled over like a shot deer. I had lost count of the number of times it had done that since we first set out. It went skidding down the slope a short way until it dug in and stopped, but the ropes holding the keg snapped like old twine. We scrambled to grab it but were too late and watched in horror as it careered down the long incline and struck a tree. The bung popped out and the precious dark liquid gushed into the snow. Cameron and I fairly tumbled down the slope to try to salvage a cup or two, but our efforts were in vain. In the time it took us to reach it, the keg had emptied completely.

Cameron cursed our luck as we scrambled back up the slippery slope to the sled. By the time we got it righted and back on track, a few more of us were cursing too. Then, as if to prove that disasters come in threes, we discovered that all of our matches had somehow been soaked and rendered useless. If our situation was desperate before, it had suddenly become deadly.

A heatless, dying sun was skirting the tops of the trees, and the forest was suffused with a combination of long shadows and pink-tinged light that I would have thought starkly beautiful under different circumstances. The bone-numbing wind had so far not returned, for which we were grateful, and the forest was as still and silent as a mausoleum. We stopped to consider our options, which, it seemed to me, were swiftly running out. A labyrinthine forest engulfed us and provided not a single hint of a trail. Everything looked different in the snow, which was deep enough to hide any blazes that might have been cut into the trees. There was some confusion and disagreement as to where we were. Since we'd been moving with the sun to our right, I reckoned we had to be somewhere between the Swift River and Snowshoe Creek. If my estimate was correct, we were probably about six or seven miles from Davis' Crossing. In order to survive this journey, we needed to find the roadhouse there as quickly as possible. That frightening fact had escaped none of my companions.

After some discussion, we concluded that one man with a good sense of direction should go ahead, unencumbered, to find the roadhouse and thus establish a trail that the rest could follow. When I asked who would do this, not a single one of my companions volunteered. To a man, they were afraid they'd get lost, and in doing so place all our lives in jeopardy. They were, however, not without an alternative, and turned their eyes toward me.

"You could find it," they said.

It ruffled me that they would place such an onerous responsibility upon my youthful shoulders. I was reasonably sure that I knew where we were, but it was only instinct and not absolute knowledge. Dr. Wilkinson, who had been with us from the start, and Cameron took me aside.

"You must go," they pleaded. "You are our best bet."

Such was the desperation in their eyes that I did not dare refuse. It was my youth and stamina that was needed, along with what they believed was an unerring sense of direction. It flashed across my mind that if an ability to accept responsibility was in truth the measure of a man, as my father had so often told me, then like it or not, I was about to be measured. And like it or not, I would have to stand up to it even if it meant perishing in the attempt.

"Will you go?" Cameron asked, and I replied with much more confidence than I felt, "Yes, I will, and I'll find it too. You needn't worry. I won't make the least mistake."

Never a man to mince words, Dr. Wilkinson said bluntly, "If you do, we are all dead men."

I struck out over snow that had had some time to settle, so at least it wasn't fighting me every step of the way. I paced myself to conserve energy, keeping the red ball of the sinking sun on my right shoulder. When it disappeared, and the forest dimmed, I kept there the waning light on the horizon. Soon, even the twilight had faded and I trudged on under a ghostly light cast by a gibbous moon on the white mantle of snow. Then I came upon a wide cut in the trees and sensed a vague familiarity about it, even in the gloom. I had passed this way before in better times, of that I was certain. It must be, it had to be, the head-waters of Snowshoe Creek and that meant I hadn't much farther to go.

I descended as quickly as my snowshoes would allow, down the frozen, twisting channel, my confidence waxing and wan-ing with the rounding of each bend. The soft contours of the pale snow hid the sharp angles of boulders and deadfalls, and glimmering stars lit the heavens. The moon seemed to pull at me the way it does the sea, drawing me down the white-and-black corridor so that I felt momentarily mesmerized. Despite my precarious situation it seemed a lovely place, and the thought crossed my mind that if I stayed there forever it would not be such a bad thing. Then I reached a larger stream that I knew for certain was Keithley Creek, and it returned me to my senses. I turned down it, and soon, like a miracle, there was a faint smell of wood smoke in the air. I sniffed it as if it were the most expensive perfume in the world, daubed on the neck of a woman of extraordinary beauty. Minutes later I was bang-ing on the door of the roadhouse at Davis' Crossing.

The old German who owned the place greeted me with much surprise that someone would be arriving at his door at so late an hour in the dead of winter, especially someone travelling alone. A log fire blazed on the hearth and the room felt uncomfortably warm. I told my story, which, since time was crucial, spilled past my lips rather quickly. The old man insisted that I eat some-thing before I go, then wasted not a moment in loading me up with bread, meat and matches. He wished me well as he saw me out the door into the frozen night, and I headed back through the slit in the forest wall to find my companions.

I worried about them as I retraced my tracks back up the creek. Cold is a seductress who makes it easy for a man to fall into her arms. She seems to promise sleep and warmth, but it is only death in an alluring disguise. Luckily, no such fate had befallen any of our party and we met up about two miles from the roadhouse. They were practically crawling along, barely able to discern my tracks well enough to follow them. Concerned only for their survival, they had abandoned the coffin soon after we'd parted company, and were travelling light, one man carrying the blankets and another the gold. Never had I known a group of men so glad to see me. They crowded around and Cameron grabbed my hand.

"God bless you, Stevenson," he exulted. "You have saved our lives!"

While I gathered up some wood and got a good fire going, the others wolfed down some of the food I'd brought. Everyone was in high spirits, which might have been improved only by an ounce or two of the excellent Hudson's Bay rum we'd left colouring the snow several miles back. We spent a restful night in that brutally cold wilderness, grateful to be alive, and at daybreak, went back for the coffin. Without serious mishap, we coaxed it down to Davis' Crossing, though it took us till long after nightfall.

The following morning, we descended to the mouth of Keithley Creek where there was a small store and a house. We bade farewell to eight more men who returned to Richfield, including Dr. Wilkinson. French Joe and Indian Jim elected to stay on and help until the danger of smallpox was imminent.

From Keithley Creek there was a well-established trail to Quesnelle Forks, and the going was much easier. Together, we pushed and pulled the sled, righting it every time it fell over, for a dozen miles or more until at last we were dropping down the winding, precarious hill into the Forks.

Queer stories abound in Cariboo, but perhaps one of the queerest was that of Mrs. Lawless, the owner of the hotel at which we found lodging. That was not her real name. Many people knew her as Johanna Maguire, but that was apparently a pseudonym too. She spoke with an Irish accent that belonged to the peasant class and I've never heard such profanity pour forth from the mouth of a woman, before or since. She mixed easily with men and could drink with the worst of us, often

Quesnelle Forks during the 1880s. (Courtesy of BC Archives A-04045)

leaving a few gasping for air. Her most recent name, Mrs. Lawless, was in one sense very fitting, for she was a wild and reckless person who cared little for any form of protocol. She ignored all inquiries into her past, and for the longest time no one knew a thing about her — where in Ireland she had come from, or what circumstances had brought her to the colonies in the first place. Then one day David Higgins, a newspaper reporter who, years later, would become a good friend of mine, discovered that she wasn't who she said she was.

Higgins, who was much more jovial and down to earth than his serious countenance indicated, was living in Yale and acting as an agent for the express service that delivered the mail; one day a woman with a broad Irish accent walked in to ask if there was any mail for "Johanna Maguire." There was, a letter bearing a Dublin postmark and containing a five-pound note. After that she came in weekly to inquire and sometimes there was a letter and sometimes not. But each time there was one, it contained a five-pound note.

It seemed to my friend that she must surely have come from the lowest of classes, for her speech gave every indication that she was lacking any sort of formal education. She held wild orgies in her cabin at the edge of Yale, and wouldn't hesitate to break a chair over a rowdy miner's head if the situation demanded it. She also "swore like a trooper," he said, and if anybody had asked him to "point out a thoroughly depraved and worthless person," he would have pointed immediately at Johanna Maguire.

But Johanna Maguire was a woman with a secret.

Not long afterwards, Higgins accompanied a doctor to the home of a sick child. It was a single-room cabin and the child's bed was partitioned off behind a curtain. The two men heard a sweet, cultivated woman's voice reciting the Lord's Prayer. Drawing back the curtain, they discovered Johanna Maguire at the child's bedside. She immediately started talking in her heavy brogue, and when asked where the woman was who had recited the prayer, answered, "She hopped out the windey as ye come in." Then Maguire ran from the room.

Three weeks later, Higgins was out for a walk when he heard a woman yelling that a man was drowning in the river. He ran to offer assistance and encountered Johanna Maguire. She was in an extremely excited state and spoke perfect English. Once the incident had passed and she had calmed down, however, she resorted to her brogue and cursed Higgins.

The next time they saw each other was at police court in Victoria in 1861. She had gotten drunk with a consort who then beat her badly. The judge asked for background information about her, but she refused to talk. He then threatened her with 60 days in jail for contempt of court. Unfazed by the threat, she responded, "I would not tell you if you gave me my natural life!" What's more, she dropped all charges against her attacker.

Afterwards, a doctor was called to her home. Her injuries from the beating were so bad that she thought she might die. She had a legal advisor there, a friend of Higgins', to whom she confessed her early history. She spoke all the while with an educated, cultured accent. Surviving the beating, she left town and Higgins thought she'd gone south. But she'd gone north instead and was running the hotel in Quesnelle Forks under the name of Lawless. And surprisingly, she was the long-lost daughter of the great Irish "Liberator" himself, Daniel O'Connell![1]

Of course, I didn't find that out until many years later, but it didn't surprise me that Mr. O'Connell could sire such a wild creature, considering the philanderer that he was. Whatever the case, I never for a moment doubted her Irish heritage. Like her fellow countrymen in general — I too am descended from them — and her supposed father in particular, she had the gift of the tongue. And like a politician, she was never afraid to use it. She spent much of her loquacity that night trying to persuade us to return to Williams Creek. To go any farther, she maintained, would be foolhardy. Smallpox was on a rampage that began just south of the Forks and continued all the way along our route to Port Douglas.

"'Tis only a dead body ye're transportin'," she said. "Is that worth riskin' yer own skins?"

Cameron did not answer her — could not answer her — for it would require words he was unable to speak in that company. Besides, such consequences were of little concern to him and he would carry on as long as he had help. So he merely shrugged and looked at me.

"There is no question of turning back," I said.

When we left the following morning, Mrs. Lawless was even firmer in her resolve that we should not go on. We were just as firm that we should. We struck out for Beaver Lake, some 15 miles to the south, and arrived there after the supper hour, having experienced the usual annoyances with the unstable sled as we descended into the broad valley containing the lake. It was February 10 and so far, we had been on the trail 11 days, yet we had covered only 72 miles. But we were moving faster now, over better roads, which was a good thing, for French Joe and Indian Jim had reached the end of the trail. In the morning, they would return to Richfield. Meanwhile, the weather remained frigid, with overnight temperatures between 40 and 50 below.

Beaver Lake was a white field of death. The area undulated with small mounds, all snow graves. By that I mean the bodies underneath had not been properly interred and were covered only with snow until the spring thaw when the graves could be excavated. Smallpox had struck the local Indian tribe and wiped out every man, woman and child, except for one bewildered old man. Altogether, I counted 90 graves, but there may have been more that I couldn't see.

Cameron dug into the gold poke and bought a horse, a sturdy mare, and a harness rig for $300. Granted, it was expensive, but as far as we were concerned it was money well spent. We hitched the sled to the animal and set off, with me leading and Cameron following behind. Down through Deep Creek and Williams Lake the snow wasn't much more than a couple of feet deep, not counting the drifts; nevertheless, the horse struggled with the load, which kept digging in and upsetting. There were signs of smallpox everywhere. Small Indian villages devastated by the disease were eerily characterized by the ubiquitous hummocks of snow. At Williams Lake I counted 120, and found only three Indians alive. They were a sorry-looking lot, as silent as the graves they stood beside as we passed by.

All through the Lac la Hache Valley, the story was repeated. We stopped at old Mr. Wright's place and there were two snow graves just a few feet from his door. One was an Indian, he said, who had died of the smallpox and the other was a white man, a murder victim. According to Mr. Wright, the man had worked for a local settler and got into a fight with another employee over a game of cards. As the two men fought, one picked up a stool and beat the other to death with it. The murderer rode off and had not been seen since.

The miles went by comparatively fast now. The road was much improved, but it was still a hard grind that kept us hot and sweating as it twisted and turned, descending into deep hollows and rising up killing grades. Given the slightest excuse the sled would tip over and was the scourge of our existence. There was evidence of smallpox all the way down the road, so much that I gave up counting the snow graves. (The year 1862 was the worst of the smallpox epidemic, and by 1864, it had claimed about 20,000 Indians.) With surprising ease we took the long hill down into 100 Mile House and continued on, passing roadhouses every 10 to 15 miles. The road then made a long and gradual ascent to a rolling tableland, among snow-laden spruce and frozen lakes.

The horse began to struggle with the weight of the load and slowed down alarmingly, steam rising from her rump. Near 70 Mile House, she stopped altogether and refused to move another step. No amount of coaxing would budge her. Suddenly she collapsed to her knees, paused for a moment, then fell over onto the snow. She lay there panting, then her breathing slowed, her eyes rolled back in her head and she died.[2] Cameron and I undid the harness and shafts and got between them ourselves, but we made a poor pair of draft animals. Even between the two of us, we had nowhere near the strength of a single horse and the strain on our backs and shoulders was prodigious. Fortunately, the last stretch of road was downhill and we made the next roadhouse before almost falling over dead ourselves. Cameron wasted no time in opening the poke to buy another horse, this time a rather ragged-looking chestnut stallion.

From 70 Mile House the road, still undulating, tended to descend rather consistently as we left the high land behind and we passed along it quite quickly. Soon, even the Great Chasm was at our backs. Every mile seemed to bring an improvement in the road, which was now in excellent condition and quite level from side to side. We reached 47 Mile House, which is now called Clinton, with relative ease.

Beyond the house the road turned southwest and remained fairly level for several miles as it ran along the floor of Cut-Off Valley and past a frozen lake. From there we could see it snaking its way toward the top of Pavilion Mountain. In fact, it looked so much like a serpent as it wound its way in six sweeping turns up the flank of the mountain that it had been named "Rattlesnake Grade." Here and there, it stuck out over the appallingly steep mountainside on platforms supported by a

The Great Chasm, 13 miles north of Clinton. (COURTESY OF BC ARCHIVES G-00790)

cribwork of wooden beams. Cameron and I had crossed this mountain before, albeit much less encumbered, and knew it for the barrier that it was. The ease of travel we'd been enjoying for several miles had come to a decidedly abrupt end.

As we began our ascent up that slippery, narrow trail, my one fervent wish was for a railing, any kind of railing, that would act as a buffer to prevent us from plummeting to our deaths. But there was nothing except empty space, so we hugged the mountainside as if we desired to become part of it. The morning had broken a dull grey and now a light, grainy snow began to fall while a variable wind picked up and blew the flakes helter-skelter. Thank God it did not worsen and the visibility remained fair. Cameron and I took turns leading the horse, while the other pushed the sled from behind and tried to keep it from tumbling over the edge. Looking down in places made my stomach flutter. Our snowshoes proved useless on the hard-packed snow so we removed them. Still, I lost track of the times our feet skidded out from under us and we fell flat on our faces. And every time we fell it not only put a greater load on the horse, but it sapped our own rapidly dwindling strength even more as we struggled back to our feet. The horse strained up the grade with the heavy load, far more sure-footed than either Cameron or I, but still with great difficulty. We rested the animal and ourselves often, but every step up that long, steep road was a contest between ourselves and the mountain. When we reached the top all three of us were about done in.

Our altitude gain must have been at least 2,000 feet with the mountaintop well over 5,000 feet above sea level. Even with the weather conditions, the view was panoramic. Before us, the road began a modest descent to a flat, snow-covered expanse that

This drawing of Rattlesnake Grade by Walter Cheadle is highly stylized, affected, no doubt, by his own hair-raising experience on it in 1862. Standing at the head of Kelly Lake today, it is impossible to see the road because of the trees. In Stevenson's and Cheadle's day, however, the road was new and many of the trees had been cut down for cribbing, firewood and brakes.

(FROM *CHEADLE'S JOURNAL OF A TRIP ACROSS CANADA*)

sloped away gently to our right for some distance before falling off rather dramatically toward the Fraser River. It was as if the gods had taken pity on us for our recent exhausting toil and were rewarding us with easy travel for the time being. The wind was strong and bitter but it was on our backs and despite our lassitude, we set a good pace to a roadhouse about four miles from the Rattlesnake Grade.

We were now only 29 miles from Lillooet, but from where we were on that plateau, surrounded by snow-covered mountain peaks, it might have been a million. I've never been one to complain, but on that night I was grateful a roadhouse existed in such a lonely place, that a cheery fire crackled in its fireplace, and that we were sheltered from the arctic wind that howled unhindered across the mountaintop. The warmth and wavering light offered by the fire were as comforting as our host was welcoming. Still, I found the utter isolation of that spot, so high above everything else, to be strangely unsettling, though I am at a loss to explain why, for I have seen worse. As weary as I felt, I looked forward to the morning when we could leave that desolation behind. Our host sensed my impatience and suggested that I not be so eager. Some of those 29 miles to Lillooet, he assured me, might very well have me wishing I hadn't left the sanctuary of his roadhouse.

The grey light of the morning saw us some three miles across the flat top of the mountain to the perilous trail that zigzagged down to the valley floor 1,500 feet below. This trail was much steeper than the Rattlesnake Grade and both Cameron and I thanked our lucky stars that we weren't travelling in the opposite direction with his wife's coffin. We might not have made it up that grade with two horses, let alone one. Still, going down provided its own set of challenges. We had to be extremely careful, lest we found ourselves taking a much faster route to the bottom than we would have liked. The owner of the roadhouse had told us that wagon-masters negotiating the downgrade in the summertime would drag heavy logs behind their rigs, like sea anchors, to act as brakes. From what I could see, there was little cause to doubt him. That stretch would have been dangerous enough in summer, never mind in winter when it was slick with ice and snow.

At the top of the hill there was a pile of logs awaiting the wagons in the spring. We selected a small one and tied it to the sled, then with some trepidation started down the three-mile slope, the pitch so steep in places that we seemed in constant danger of losing everything over the side, including ourselves. On the hairpin curves we looped a rope around the rear stanchions of the runners and eased the sled around the corner by pulling it in toward the mountainside. The blunt end of the log kept digging into the snow, working as a brake, and kept the sled from getting away on us. It was excruciatingly difficult work and the tension on our backs, particularly on the backs of our legs, was punishing. We panted and groaned down that grade for a dog's age before we got to the bottom. By that time my legs were trembling from fatigue. Cameron looked completely worn out and more dour than usual but voiced not a single complaint, though at his age I'd wager he felt worse than I.

We did precisely what our bodies begged us not to do and pressed on, demanding no less from the horse. Much of the rest of the day slipped by in a fog and just as the sky, which had remained a dull grey the entire day, was giving up to darkness, we came to a roadhouse, high above the Fraser River and some 15 miles from Lillooet. By that time, neither man nor beast was fit for another inch of travel.

As we prepared for our departure the next morning we found much consolation in the fact that Pavilion Mountain was a good distance behind us and a small town with decent food and drink was not far ahead. The road down the Fraser was relatively wide and in good shape so we pushed hard, hoping to reach Lillooet before nightfall. Following the course of the river, the road rose and fell in waves as it wound in great looping turns among the folds of the steep, sagebrush-covered hillsides. In places it left the river to run straight across fairly level benches that provided temporary relief from the strain of traversing the road's many undulations. The closer we got to Lillooet the more forested the hillsides became, while the rocky outcrops gleamed red in the light of a welcome sun.

The horse grew winded, as did we, but we forced him on and by suppertime were moving gingerly down a long switchback that descended gradually to the river's edge. A winch ferry sat there, as if waiting expressly for us, and we rode the current across the narrow channel to the far side. Climbing up the opposite bank to the terrace upon which Lillooet sat was a Herculean struggle for the horse, but we drove him on without remorse, thrashing his rump with a stripped branch. Somehow, the poor beast made it to the top of the hill, though Cameron muttered doubts that he would make it all the way into town, which was now within hailing distance up the road. My legs felt rubbery and weak and I said a silent prayer of thanks that the day's journey was nearly at an end.

If the spectre of smallpox hanging over it was disregarded, Lillooet was an oasis in a desert of snow. The main street was wide enough to turn a team of oxen around in, and, even better, it was smooth and level. There were more than a dozen saloons, which seemed an extraordinary number for a town its size, but we managed to find a livery stable among them and put the horse up for the night. We took rooms at the Stage

Hotel and were late for supper, but the cook took pity on us and warmed up some leftover potatoes, salted ham, biscuits and gravy that we washed down with several cups of scalding coffee. Then, for the first time on our journey, we slept in a proper bed.

Lest it be thought that the roadhouses we'd stopped at were as respectable as the Stage Hotel, let me dispel that foolish notion right now. They were, for the most part, hovels — usually single-roomed log cabins with a fireplace at one end and a countertop at the other — that offered little more than a place out of the wind and rain in summer, and a modest opportunity to reduce the risk of frostbite in winter. And I never stayed in one that wasn't also inhabited by a large population of lice and bedbugs. In fact, the miners often held racing competitions with the vermin; they were placed on plates and the first to reach the far side was the winner.

We slept on the floor, which might have been fine had the floors been smooth, but mostly they were rough-hewn planks with more lumps in them than a dried-up stream bed. The smooth beds were the countertops — if the house had any. We were lucky in one respect, though. Since there were few travellers on the road in winter, we were always able to get a space next to the fire. However, the draught coming in under the door was usually enough to keep one side of our bodies in a frozen condition all night.

Few miners would disagree with me when I say that in the beginning, the only thing remotely comforting in those houses was the liquor. After a hard day's slog on the trail, it would send a most joyous flood of warmth and well-being through your entire body, provided, of course, you were able to get it

Walter Cheadle's rendition of the interior of a Cariboo Trail roadhouse.
(FROM *CHEADLE'S JOURNAL OF A TRIP ACROSS CANADA*)

past your lips. I would not be stretching the truth to say that much of it tasted as if it was distilled by the Devil himself. I disparage here the rot-gut whiskey and rum that was prevalent up and down the trail, and not the fine Hudson's Bay products. Yet good or bad, its quality had no bearing on the price. All of it cost a king's ransom.

At the livery stable in the morning, the owner informed us that our horse was not likely to survive the day, let alone the rest of our journey. That news held no surprise for either of us. We opened up the gold poke and bought another, for the one thing we could not do without was a horse. The stable owner assured us the animal was a fine one, hardy enough to get our cargo all the way to Port Douglas. He therefore charged us accordingly.

We set off before first light in deep snow. It was only a few miles to Seton Lake, which was covered in places by a thin, watery layer of ice, though not enough to stop the small paddlewheeler that plied its length. It bore us swiftly down the lake between steep mountains that plunged straight into the dark green depths. At the far end, a small tram on wooden rails carried us and our cargo over a short portage connecting Seton with Anderson Lake, and we were soon steaming down the latter's dark waters against a light chop. The vessel moved slowly, taking three hours to run the 16-mile length of the lake.

We stayed that night at a roadhouse run by a loquacious Frenchman who charged us two dollars each for our meals and beds and a dollar for livery for the horse. This was expensive as roadhouses go, but he kept a clean establishment and for that we were grateful. I was curious about a marker out behind the house and was told it was the grave of a Mexican killed in a brawl the summer before. This had been during an extraordinarily busy period, when miners vied to be first on the creeks and tempers were easily ignited. But these were quieter times, with Cameron and me the only travellers. We each enjoyed a jug of mulled wine to celebrate the easiest day of travel we had had so far, then turned in.

There was much less snow on the ground from that point on and the air temperature was substantially warmer. Neither of these improvements, however, did anything to prevent the sled from pitching onto its side at the slightest provocation. It was a long, tough pull amongst the thickly forested mountains and over some pretty rugged terrain that more than made up for the ease of the previous day's travel. By late afternoon, we caught a glimpse of wood smoke rising from Ketterel's Halfway House,

Ketterel's Halfway House in 1865, nestled among the mountains on the Pemberton-Anderson Lake portage. (COURTESY OF BC ARCHIVES G-00793)

but it seemed a disproportionately long time before the building itself appeared on the far side of a rocky hillock.

Compared to the roadhouses north of Lillooet, places like Ketterel's were relatively luxurious, providing good food, good drink and comfortable beds to sleep in. Unless, of course, a traveller arrived during the busy season, in which case he'd find himself sleeping on the floor if he wanted a roof over his head for the night. But while there were other customers besides Cameron and me, they were few in number and we were able to obtain beds.

After a good night's sleep, we were off early and moved quickly through to Pemberton, the last few miles being flat as a billiard table. Peter Smith's roadhouse at Pemberton was a fine establishment and, like Ketterel's, was an indication of how accommodations along this route were changing for the better. The barkeeper was a young man named Richard Alexander, who was one of the Overlanders of 1862. He had some hair-raising tales to tell of his arduous journey across the continent from Canada, particularly down the Fraser River, which had swallowed up one of his companions. He was disappointed that he had arrived too late in the mining season to find his fortune, and ended up instead doing menial work to survive the winter. But he was optimistic — an indispensable quality for any miner — and was determined to be one of the first on the creeks when they opened up in the spring. I believe he was, but ultimately it didn't do him a lick of good. He stayed only for a season and left like most miners did — with lots of experience and not much else. The last I heard, he was managing a sawmill in Vancouver.

At the roadhouse there was another man, who had just finished digging a coal pit for Smith. His name was Jim Cummings, and though he'd spent the summer on Williams Creek, we hadn't met before. Cameron asked him about the road to Port Douglas. It was in reasonably good shape, Cummings said, adding that he was about to embark upon it himself come the morning, bound for New Westminster. Cameron thought that an extra hand wouldn't hurt our circumstances a bit and suggested we travel together. We'd pay him five dollars a day for his help and look after his expenses to boot. Cummings eagerly agreed.

Alexander sent us off in the morning with a good lunch that he'd packed. We hauled the sled down to the steamboat landing on Lillooet Lake and boarded the *Prince of Wales*, which took us down to the Douglas Portage. Once we got onto it, the road was accommodatingly wide and in better shape than we'd expected. We made good time until the afternoon when conditions worsened and the surface hardened with ice. We slipped and staggered down the treacherous track, Cameron using his axe to cut stakes that he used at the side of the sled to prevent it from sliding off the shoulder. While I led the horse, Cummings helped Cameron but in places, our progress was painstakingly slow. Several times the stakes proved useless and the sled went off the road anyway. But we'd seen it turn turtle so many times by then that it had long ceased to bother us. Cummings hadn't, though, and his frustration showed. Finally, he suggested that he carry the gold on his back, which would make the load less top-heavy. That seemed like a good idea to me as well as to Cameron and we quickly agreed. From then on, there were fewer problems trying to keep the sled upright.

We reached 20 Mile House shortly after dark and whiled away the evening soothing our weary muscles in the mineral hot springs over which a part of the house was built. (The roadhouses along this portion of the route were named according to the mileage from Port Douglas. The Cariboo roadhouses, at 47, 70, 100, and 150 miles, were measured from Lillooet.) The next day, with the weather favourable and the road in excellent condition, we pushed on to Port Douglas at the top end of Harrison Lake, and got there before daylight was spent. We'd come to the end of the overland part of our journey, which might have been good cause for celebration had it not been for the horrific sight that greeted our eyes as we entered the community.

Both sides of the road were lined with tents, and the door flaps were turned back far enough to allow us a glimpse of their occupants. We saw Indians in just about every stage of small-pox that could be imagined, some so far gone their skin had turned black. The stink of the dead and the dying hung in the air like dust on a windless day, so thick it seemed to embrace us. My God, how my stomach turned! We hurried by, fearing the air itself was poisoned, hiding our faces in the crooks of our arms so that we wouldn't have to breathe it. Though nearly 60 years have passed since the events related here, I need only close my eyes to relive that sickening scene. I see it and smell it, and it is no less horrible than it was back then.

We were now less than a hundred miles from New Westminster, all of which could be travelled by boat. The next morning, for the last time, we hitched the sled to the horse and made our way to the small paddlewheeler *Henrietta*, tied up at

The community of Port Douglas, much as Stevenson and Cameron saw it, except for the tents and the horror they contained. (COURTESY OF BC ARCHIVES A-03519)

the lake's edge. We left the horse under the care of the roadhouse owner, and gave him the sled as a gift. Then we hoisted the coffin on rope slings strung between two poles and carried it on board. When the whistle blew and the vessel eased away from the landing, I could scarcely believe our travail was all but over.

The journey down Harrison Lake was as pleasant a boat ride as I'd ever taken. We had an ample supply of Hudson's Bay brandy to pass the time and cared not a whit when a shaft to the paddlewheel broke. While the engineer worked feverishly to repair it, we drifted down the lake when the wind was favourable, and nudged into shore when it wasn't. During those periods, Captain Millard had the strange habit of ordering the Indians in his crew up the closest mountainside to roll down the biggest rocks they could find. When Cummings inquired into this curious command, the captain replied it was done to keep the Indians in good health.

Once the shaft was repaired, the captain put on extra steam to an overnight anchorage near the hot springs. The next day's end saw us offloading our cargo on the pier at New Westminster, notable only for its lack of snow.

Cameron had plans to buy another claim once he was in Victoria and asked Cummings if it could be put in his name. In those days a man couldn't legally own more than two claims (the one he originally staked, plus one that he bought) so it was the only way Cameron could expand his holdings. Cummings agreed with great enthusiasm, provided he could work it at a foreman's wage. They shook hands and promised to meet back in New Westminster a few days hence.

The steamer *Enterprise* departed at first light the following day and we were happily aboard it, our precious cargo under canvas and lashed securely to the foredeck. The weather was turning sour just as we rounded Ogden Point, too late to cause us any grief, and the coffin was soon being winched onto a wet and windswept Hudson's Bay wharf in Victoria harbour. It was Friday, March 6, nearly five weeks after we'd left Williams Creek.

Chapter Eight

WE WENT STRAIGHT away to the Royal Hotel where the Wilcoxes greeted us as if we were family. Sophia's coffin was stored for the night in the same back room her daughter had occupied almost exactly a year ago. This had a visible effect on Cameron, yet he said nothing.

Before calling it a night, Cameron and I walked up to the Boomerang for a hot whiskey. Victoria had changed remarkably over the past year. It had grown in size, but most notable were the new brick buildings and the gas lamps lighting some of the streets. There was no less mud, of course, but the boardwalks and crosswalks were more plentiful and in much better condition. More numerous, too, were the faces we saw pitted by smallpox.

Richard Lewis was the undertaker who had attended to Mary Isabella Alice, so our first order of business in the morning was to visit his premises. Though Sophia's body was still in a frozen state, it wouldn't remain that way for very long. If Cameron was to fulfil his promise, her body needed somehow to be preserved so that it could be transported through the hot tropical

131

climate of Panama and the Caribbean. Mr. Lewis had the perfect solution. Alcohol, he said, would do the job, but it had to be at least 95 proof, and at least 25 gallons would be required. It wouldn't be inexpensive, he added, but since the interior coffin was already made of tin, it would be more than adequate to contain the liquid and preserve the remains. To Cameron, of course, price was no object and he instructed Lewis to do whatever was necessary to see the job through. We left after arranging to meet him later that morning at the Royal.

Just before noon, the undertaker's wagon pulled up in front of the hotel. He had with him a large keg of alcohol and a tinsmith, a lanky man in ill-fitting clothes wearing a bowler hat and sporting an enormous moustache. Together we moved the keg to the room containing Sophia's remains. The wooden lid was carefully removed and the tradesman cut a small hole through the top of the sealed tin coffin. Over the next two and a half hours, Lewis carefully poured the alcohol through the opening, ewer upon ewer, until it bubbled over the top. With a rag, he mopped up the excess liquid and had the tinsmith seal the hole. We could do nothing more but wait for the funeral.

Meanwhile, Cameron and I had become celebrities around town. News of our huge gold strike had preceded our arrival and it seemed everyone was eager to either talk to us or at least catch a glimpse of us, so that they could tell their friends. And speaking of friends, we discovered we had more than we had ever known about, and many people scrambled over each other in a bid to win our favour. An indication of our new-found popularity was the size of Sophia's funeral cortege on Sunday, which was not surpassed in that century until they buried Sir James Douglas in 1877. Then there was the amount of space

Christ Church Cathedral, 1860s. (COURTESY OF BC ARCHIVES A-02555)

devoted to Sophia in the *British Colonist* on Monday. She had gone from relative obscurity to the limelight simply by being the dead wife of a rich man. I have kept that clipping over the years and offer it here in its entirety:

Mrs. J. A. Cameron's Funeral — The remains of this deeply lamented lady were removed from the Royal Hotel on Wharf street yesterday at half past three o'clock, and followed to the grave at Christ Church Cemetery by the largest and most respectable funeral cortege which we have ever witnessed in the city. In addition to the whole mining community at present in town, there was a vast number of our principal inhabitants who came unsolicited to pay respects to the memory of the deceased, as well as to manifest the sympathy which they felt for her husband under his terrible affliction. The funeral passed up Yates

133

street, along Government street, and thence by Fort street to the cemetery, where the Rev. Mr. Pall, Presbyterian minister to whose Communion both the deceased and her husband belonged, conducted the solemn service. In a touching and extremely appropriate address the Reverend gentleman with great earnestness dwelt upon the faithfulness and womanly devotion of the deceased to her husband, how she left her happy home to follow his fortunes to the mountain ranges of an inhospitable country, the loss of her promising babe in this city just one year since, and how nobly she risked her health and ease to contribute to the comfort of him she loved.

Mrs. Cameron was the daughter of Mr. Nathan Groves of Stormont in the county of Cornwall, C.W., and was quite a young woman. During her residence in this city before going to Cariboo, she was highly respected and wherever she went she endeared herself to all with whom she came in contact by her genial disposition and benevolence of spirit. During her long and severe confinement before her death not a murmur escaped her lips and her sole thought was for him from whom she was so soon to be separated.

Deeply attached to her in life Mr. Cameron has not forgotten the respect due to her remains, as with a heroism which is not often met with, he boldly faced the rigors of an almost arctic winter and brought the corpse a distance of 600 miles, at an expense of nearly $2,000, to have it interred with the rites of christian burial. Besides, so deeply rooted was his attachment to the deceased that he intends to have her remains, with that of their child, exhumed and taken to Canada for interment in the family burying ground. It was a singular coincidence that on yesterday [it was] just twelve months since the child was interred in the same grave in which the remains of the mother have now been laid, and within an hour of the same time of day. Mrs. Cameron was attended in her last illness by Dr. Wilkinson, who left nothing untried which might tend to his patient's recovery. Alas! without effect.

The residents of Richfield turned out when Mrs. Cameron was leaving and followed in procession to the top of the mountain where they took their leave.[1] The funeral arrangements were conducted by Mr. Richard Lewis, undertaker, very creditably.

On Monday, Cameron and I had business to conduct. We repaired first to the Hudson's Bay Company warehouse where Cameron paid his debt in full, much to the trader's delight. Then we went to the government claims office where he bought a claim right next to ours, putting it in the name of James Cummings. Then we paid a visit to the Clendenning brothers who were wintering in a tent on the edge of town. They were tired of the rigours of mining, they said, not to mention life in a tent, and readily sold their shares in the original claim for what I thought was an uncommonly reasonable price. Cameron now owned more than half of it, since Sophia's share had reverted to him after her death.

Once our business was completed, we walked over to Wharf Street to where the *British Colonist* was located in a tiny, false-fronted wooden building, and Cameron placed an ad in the paper publicly thanking the Wilcoxes for their help. Then there

The British Colonist *office on Wharf Street, Victoria.*
(COURTESY OF BC ARCHIVES A-04656)

was nothing for it but to wait until Wednesday when the steamer departed for New Westminster.

Jim Cummings was waiting expectantly for our arrival, and was instructed to return to Williams Creek as fast as his obligations in town would allow. He could use the horse we'd left at Port Douglas. Then Cameron and I were away on a sternwheeler to Yale where we bought horses for $350 each and rode in comparative luxury as far as Williams Lake. From there, we went on foot, retracing our route through Quesnelle Forks, Keithley Creek, and past Tom Maloney's roadhouse. We arrived back in Richfield on April 4, 1863, having made the return journey of more than a thousand miles in just 66 days.

A few days later Cummings pulled in, having come the longer way around, via Quesnellemouth and Lightning Creek.

Chapter Nine

THE NEXT FEW months on the creek were extraordinarily hectic. The first thing that had to be done was pay back Billy Barker's loan, which we did with interest. The next was to excavate our claims until we'd taken all the gold we wanted from them. We'd only just got started when trouble came along to interrupt us.

During the first week in May, the waged workers up and down the creek went on strike. They were now earning $10 for a 10-hour day and wanted $12. We gave it to them. Then two weeks later they struck again, only this time for an 8-hour day, while still earning $12. We gave that to them also. But then it turned out that a lot of the men, particularly the strike instigators, were working double shifts on different claims while others had no work at all. As owners, we considered that practice unacceptable and shut the mines down, even though it was a drastic measure that cost everyone a lot of money, workers and owners alike. It cost the Cameron Company alone $20,000 for without attention, many of the mineshafts collapsed and had to be re-excavated.

Several meetings were held with a view to resolving the dispute, at which most felt that the best thing to do was to revert to the old system of $10 for 10 hours. But no one would put forward a motion to that end. There was an underlying fear of the strike instigators, most of whom were American, who held sway with threats of dire consequences to those who opposed them. But there were several of us who were not about to be bullied, least of all by outsiders.

We called a meeting and assured good attendance by saying that definite action was going to be taken. The response was overwhelming. Two thousand men showed up, making it necessary to hold the meeting outside. At the proper point in the proceedings I stood up and said, "I move that wages should once more revert to $10 for 10 hours, that drifters should get $12 for 10 hours, and that all those responsible for the last strike be debarred from all works for the season."

Cummings stood up to second the motion, but no one heard him amidst the roar of cheers that resounded up and down the creek. It was what the miners had been waiting to hear and they carried the motion by a huge majority. By the next day we were back at work and the rabble-rousers, the curse of every mining camp, were routed. Later that summer, the Americans' Fourth of July was a quiet and sober celebration because of it.

We'd only just got the labour problems straightened out when trouble of a different sort arrived on our doorstep. It came in the form of a man named Robert Lamont. He showed up on a warm day in early June, a sharp-faced individual with a wispy beard on a weak chin. He said he was Jim Cummings' business partner and as such wanted a half-interest in the claim that was under Cummings' name. He had the papers to prove his partnership, which Jim did not dispute anyway. For a moment it looked as if Cameron was about to lose a claim, for on paper Cummings was undoubtedly the owner and as a legitimate partner, Lamont was entitled to half. But our new friend proved to be a man of great honour. He told Lamont that he had no ownership in the claim whatsoever and that he was merely a paid employee of Cameron's. If it came down to it, he would go to court and swear that he was only holding the claim in trust for Cameron. Lamont looked set to make trouble for all of us, but backed off.

We were paying Cummings $16 a day to act as foreman, and that was more than anyone else was making on the creek. We had also entrusted him with the key to the box in which he kept the daily take of gold. If he'd had a mind to, he could have absconded with a sizable poke, but it was a testament to his good character that he didn't. With his response to Lamont, Cummings soared in my estimation. He had not only proven himself more than worthy of the trust we'd placed in him, but he was clearly worth his weight in gold.

Through it all, Williams Creek was being transformed beyond all recognition. For a mile or more up and down the valley, buildings were being thrown up daily, especially around the Cameron claims. On July 18, beneath a 70-foot flagpole that Cameron had erected, Judge Begbie officially named the settlement "Cameron Town," which was soon shortened to "Cameronton."[1] After the ceremony, there was a party to end all parties with the Cameron claim footing the bill. If headaches were gold, there wouldn't have been a poor man anywhere in town on the following morning.

Less than a week later tragedy struck our company. Peter Gibson died. I had known him for years, and he was a good

The ruins of the Cameron cabin, Williams Creek. This is probably not the Richfield cabin in which Sophia died, but one that was built later in Cameronton. (FROM WALKEM'S *STORIES OF EARLY BRITISH COLUMBIA*)

man. He hailed from Vankleek Hill, about 25 miles north of my hometown. When my parents first came to Canada they bought a farm near the Hill and for a while Gibson and I attended the same parochial school. He had come to Rock Creek when I was there, and finding no prospects, eventually ended up as my deputy in Osoyoos. He survived those blackguards along the border only to be taken by mountain fever at just 31 years of age. Cummings and I carried his body up the stump-ridden hillside behind the town to a small area where the slope was gentle, and we cleared a space there and buried him. Before the year was out there would be more burials on that hillside and it would become our official cemetery.[2]

Those summer days were long in more ways than one. We worked the claims 24 hours a day with nearly a hundred employees and the sweat that rolled from us could have created a new creek. The days took on a rhythm that, except for a few incidents of little consequence, remained unbroken. The only discernible difference between night and day was the amount of available light. And while other claims along the creek were left wanting, every bucket we pulled up on the windlass contained staggering amounts of gold. Our good luck and punctures in the earth had made us rich beyond our wildest imaginings.

By summer's end, we had washed more than $300,000 worth of gold, over and above our expenses, a figure that included the

The Cameron claim during the summer of 1863. Cameron is sitting down in front, holding a gold pan, while Stevenson is sitting just to the left of the post. Jim Cummings is standing up behind them, third from the left.

(COURTESY OF BC ARCHIVES A-03812)

$100,000 that Jim Cummings handed over in a strongbox from his claim.[3] We made plans to return to the coast to tend to the unfinished business there, then threw a party for all the men that set Cameron back $1,000. After that, all we had to do was get our treasure to Victoria through territory that provided an infinite number of places for robbers to hide in ambush.

There was an official Gold Escort operating between Williams Creek and Victoria, comprised of 15 well-armed and well-mounted men, but they still got robbed and if they didn't, sometimes the gold conveniently got lost. Most of the miners figured they were better off creating their own escort and travelling with it, and that's what Cameron did. He hired 20 trustworthy men and armed them to the teeth with orders to shoot

A Gold Escort about to leave Barkerville in 1862.
(COURTESY OF BC ARCHIVES I-31594)

anything that looked even remotely like a bandit. Begbie warned him of the possibility of murder charges, but Cameron wasn't to be swayed. Anyone who made even the slightest wrong move was as good as dead, and damn the consequences. On October 6 a pack train of eight horses, the escort, Cameron, his two brothers who had joined us to work the claim, and I, set out on the long journey to the coast.

There was no mistaking what we were about as we plodded down that interminable road, nor was there any mistaking the seriousness of the escort. They were a hard-looking lot who would have made anybody considering a hold-up think twice about the consequences. We took turns riding ahead, checking out any likely ambush spots, but our fears were unfounded: the entire journey was made unmolested. In New Westminster, we stopped only long enough to melt the gold down into bars and then left for Victoria.

There was much work to be done upon our arrival. We went first to Richard Lewis, the undertaker who had tended to Sophia, and Cameron instructed him to make arrangements to exhume her body, along with that of their daughter. Sophia's coffin was then to be stripped down to the tin casing and a new cover of wood built for it. A new coffin for Mary Isabella Alice was ordered also. On November 8 both coffins and the gold, still under a heavily armed guard, were winched aboard the coastal steamer *Pacific* and we sailed from Victoria, bound for home with a cargo both bitter and sweet.[1]

The voyage was uneventful, if such a word can be used to describe being tossed around by heavy seas in leaky vessels for several weeks. Along the way we stopped in San Francisco long enough to convert the bullion into coin, then boarded a steamer for Panama. After a hot and humid railroad trip across the isthmus of Panama and a wild steamer journey north, dawn saw us creeping into New York's busy harbour through the veil of an early-morning snowfall. The worst of our journey may have been over, but we weren't out of the woods just yet.

We became entangled in a bureaucratic web that snagged us so tightly I thought we might never shake loose. The customs officials were immediately suspicious of Sophia's coffin because of its tremendous weight. Why, they asked pointedly, was it so heavy? Because, Cameron explained, it was filled to the brim with alcohol. Then why couldn't they hear the alcohol sloshing around inside? It was filled to capacity, Cameron replied patiently, and furthermore, his wife was swaddled in clothes so that she wouldn't be battered during the voyage.

Similar interrogations went on as Cameron and I were shuttled from office to office around the city by sympathetic hackies who each time had to be paid and appropriately tipped. At each office, the same questions were asked over and over until even we wondered if we were telling the truth. Then there were endless forms to fill out and they always required an exorbitant fee. I swore, a hundred times if I swore it once, that the coffins contained nothing more than the remains of my friend's dear departed wife and daughter, that we were merely fulfilling a deathbed promise, and that we had no intention of stopping anywhere on American soil during our railway journey to Canada West. Cameron even offered to pay the cost of a ticket for a customs official to accompany us to ensure that we spoke the truth. In fact, my friend declared with no small degree of desperation in his voice that, if the official so desired, he could come all the way to the graveyard in Glengarry and watch as

Sophia's remains were lowered into the ground and covered over for eternity. None of the customs men were willing to take their job that seriously, however, and our persistence finally won the day. We had been running around New York since eight that morning and dusk was settling over the city when we'd filled out our last form and paid our final fee. And we still hadn't got the coffin off the ship.

We hied to dockside where the steamer that had brought us the last leg of our journey was tied up. To our astonishment, the coffins were still deep within its hold, there being no winch around to hoist them out. Cameron's eyes rolled so far back in his head I thought he might never see again. One of the customs men found a long length of rope and the three of us brought up Mary's coffin. Sophia's coffin was a different matter, however. Cameron and I recruited as many seamen, dockworkers and passersby as we could by offering them two dollars each for their help. We must have had nearly a hundred men on those ropes and easily pulled the alcohol-filled coffin up onto the deck. From there it was lowered gingerly onto the back of a freight wagon, next to Mary's. The freighter followed our hack through the slippery streets to a hotel and, for a princely sum, watched over his valuable cargo throughout the long night.

The next morning we were on a train bound for Buffalo, Cameron being several hundred dollars lighter of pocket after the brief time we spent in New York. Still, I've since been led to understand that we might have fared much worse. The red tape we experienced was more likely a result of widespread graft and corruption than it was a muddled bureaucracy. It was, after all, the beginning of the era of the notorious "Boss" Tweed, whose stint as a crooked city politician is now legendary. Cameron may have been lucky to have spent only a few hundred dollars, and to get away as quickly as we did!

We finally reached Glengarry County in what is now Ontario on December 22, a year to the day since Dick Rivers had excitedly summoned us down into the mineshaft to show us his amazing discovery.

Chapter Ten

CAMERON HAD ARRIVED back home a changed man. He was older, to be sure, but he'd left the first time as a farm worker and had come back rich enough to buy the farm. It gave him an arrogance he'd not displayed before. His eyes were as direct as ever, but what was it that I saw there now? Pride for what he had achieved? Or disdain for those not as willing as he to forsake the security of their mediocre lives to pursue something greater? Perhaps it was merely defiance, a wall thrown up to hide what he truly felt about the other consequences of his single-mindedness, the ones that he was about to bury in the family plot in Cornwall.

Hundreds of mourners had gathered at the church for the funerals, the third one for Sophia Cameron, the second for Mary. It was understood why Mary's coffin would not be opened, but there was a murmur of shock among the mourners when they discovered that Sophia's wouldn't be either. As I mentioned earlier, open coffins were customary in those days, and unlike Mary's body, Sophia's had been preserved, so her family should have been allowed a final glimpse of their loved one's face, and to know for certain that she was gone from them forever. I couldn't believe that Cameron would go back on his word and deny them that opportunity. I pulled him aside and asked what was going on. I reminded him of his promise to me before we left Cariboo, that he would open the coffin.

"You gave me your word, John. Or have you forgotten?"

"I've forgotten nothing. The decision is mine to make. The coffin will remain closed."

"Damn your eyes," I seethed. "You won't get away with this. The day will come when you will have to show her face. The people are not satisfied, and never will be until you do show it. You made a distinct promise to me that you would do so, or I would never have left Cariboo with you and Sophia's remains. I have never known you to go back on your word. Why are you doing so now? This is an awful mistake you are making, John."

He looked beyond me, as if he hadn't heard a word I said, and asked if I would sign a sworn statement regarding Sophia's death. I was furious, insulted by the impudence of such a request, and refused.

"Did you know," I asked, "that someone overheard Sophia's father express misgivings that he was actually attending the funeral of his daughter since he had no idea what the coffin contains?"

Cameron snorted. "If that's true, then let whoever said that come and tell me himself!"

I didn't like his tone of voice and was going to tell him so, then thought better of it. He was beyond all reason. I fetched Aleck Robinson, the man who'd told me what Mr. Groves had said. Cameron stared into his face, those piercing eyes ablaze with anger.

"Did you hear Mr. Groves express any doubt that it's his daughter in the coffin?"

Never a man to back down from anyone, Robinson glared right back and said that that was exactly what he'd heard.

"That settles it," Cameron cried. "Now I will never show her face to anyone!"

Sophia's coffin was lowered into the ground unopened. It was obvious, from the angry and disgusted glances and whispered asides amongst the mourners, that they were not at all satisfied with Cameron's actions. He paid them no mind. The proceedings broke up with more than just a funereal pall hanging in the air.

That night at the Cameron homestead we argued till the early hours of the morning about Cameron's disturbing decision. His brothers and sisters tried several times to come between us, but I would not be appeased, and Cameron's mind would not be changed. Nor would he explain his unwillingness to co-operate.

The next day, steeped in frustration and disappointment, I left Cameron to his own side of the wall he'd built between us, and went to my parents' house. He and I had been through so much together that it bothered me deeply to part company under such unfavourable circumstances. To this day, I cannot explain why he was so adamant that the coffin remain closed. In my opinion, it was a foolish decision that succeeded in only arousing suspicion amongst Sophia's relatives and friends, and casting him in a poor light. Perhaps he couldn't bear to see again the face of a woman he had loved so deeply, a woman, I daresay, whose death he felt solely responsible for, as if he had taken a gun and shot her through the heart himself. Or maybe he was simply placed in a position where his character dictated that he should dig in his heels. I believe I have already mentioned how stubborn a man Cameron could be. Whatever the answers were, I never found out, and 25 years passed before we saw each other again.

Cameron had spent a dozen years mucking for gold, years filled with backbreaking toil and financial deprivation, and he set out to make up for them. If he saw something that he wanted, he bought it, and if it had not been for sale he offered enough money to ensure that it was. He remembered those unrewarding years working on his uncle's farm in Summerstown, how he had longed to be free of the mundane chores and their woeful lack of promise. It would be the perfect place, he thought, on which to build a home that would be fit for royalty. It didn't take much to persuade his uncle to sell the farm. Then Cameron hired others to work it for him while he oversaw the construction of his mansion.

He spared no expense, importing granite from Scotland, his ancestral homeland, marble from Italy, and exotic woods from the Philippines. He commissioned a local artisan to make and install stained-glass windows. When all was done to his satisfaction, he christened it "Fairfield." It sat overlooking the St. Lawrence River, gloating, as if it knew there was nothing to match it for miles around. And there wasn't.

In the meantime, he had a gold-trimmed carriage built for himself, then imported four beautiful grey horses from Europe to pull it around. And as if there were some longing in him to be deemed a gentleman, he rode to hounds and dressed to the nines. Then, to complete the picture, he married Christianne Emma Woods, the daughter of Colonel John Woods, a wealthy

Fairfield, Summerstown, Ontario, the house that Cameron built with his riches, as it looked in 1997. (Photo by Bill Gallaher)

neighbour. She was a capricious and giddy young woman, just 23 years old, as opposite to Sophia as ice is to steam. It was precisely these flaws that had kept her a spinster, but there was also a freshness and liveliness to her that perhaps Cameron found appealing. What's more, she was physically attractive and looked good on his arm, which may have been important to him in his masquerade as a dandy. She loved to be indulged and, as a man of extremes, he overindulged her. She proved to be the perfect hostess, and the parties they held at Fairfield were frequent, long and often quite rowdy. Their reputation for bacchanalia spread across county borders.

Yet there was no denying the man's generosity. He bought a home for his parents in Cornwall and ensured they would want for nothing during their declining years. The two brothers who had mucked with him in Cariboo were each given $40,000 and a farm, and the three brothers who chose to stay at home received $20,000 each. He lavished expensive gifts upon his sisters, too, one of them receiving a diamond-studded, 18-carat gold belt. And he would tip the most menial service worker an outrageous sum, sometimes the equivalent of a week's pay, just to see the expression on the person's face.

He used his money to create a paradise, but never understood that Edens rarely come without a resident serpent. In his case, it was gossip and innuendo. People didn't understand how Cameron could be so liberal with his money and rumours soon began to circulate that he had acquired it dishonestly. No one could have found that much gold in so short a time, they said; surely he must have obtained it by criminal means. They wondered if Sophia Cameron was actually alive, now the wife of some west coast savage, traded by her villainous husband for the gold he'd brought home. No one had forgotten his refusal to show Sophia's face at the funeral and speculation grew that there was something other than a dead body inside that coffin. Perhaps it was a great treasure? Why else would it weigh so much? The stories were whispered from mouth to ear around the community, behind Cameron's back, until late in 1865 when a local doctor went public, stating for all to hear that Cameron had indeed accumulated his fortune nefariously. Furthermore, he had even served time in jail in Cariboo for his crimes.

Cameron had had enough. He could live with the undercurrent of calumny but now it had gone too far. Since in those days recourse to the courts for such things as libel and slander was a slow and onerous procedure, he took the train to Montreal where he bought a rawhide whip. In a Cornwall hotel he confronted his accuser, fully intending to thrash the man, but before he could inflict any damage, others in the room restrained him. The doctor charged Cameron with assault and he was later found guilty. His lawyer won an appeal for a new trial but as far as I know, it never took place.

The local newspaper began to hound him. The *Cornwall Freeholder* wrote that he was a "shameless rowdy" and that "when Mr. C. assumes to introduce Lynch law into the community ... he shouldn't be surprised at the indignation .... To Mr. C. as a dandy we have nothing to say; but we can assure him that he will not be tolerated here as a ruffian .... Mr. Cameron has been away from home and like many other weak-minded persons has contracted some bad habits ...."[1]

The public outrage changed Cameron's personality even more. He grew paranoid, believing that people were only interested in him now because of his money. The short fuse on his temper became almost non-existent and he would explode at the slightest provocation. He threw guests bodily out his front door, and once heaved his brother crashing through one of Fairfield's stained-glass windows, simply for having the nerve to suggest that Cameron should do something to silence the rumour mongers once and for all by exhuming Sophia's coffin and opening it publicly.

Still he refused. And when a local judge pleaded with him to settle the questions raging across the community, Cameron seethed that his wife was resting in peace and if anyone disturbed her, he would not hesitate to kill him.

For nine years Cameron lived under an incredible strain, an exile in his own community, sustained only by his great stubbornness and perhaps a misguided belief that he was right. Then one summer day, someone brought him a copy of the

Sunday Times, a paper published down in Syracuse, New York. The story it contained was so incredible and shocking that it nearly bowled Cameron over.

A ROMANCE IN REAL LIFE. A FEAST FOR A NOVEL WRITER.
TEN YEARS WITH AN INDIAN CHIEF.
JUST RETRIBUTION.

Fifteen years ago there lived on the banks of the St. Lawrence, near the village of Cornwall, a man named Cameron of near Scotch descent. He dwelt until after maturity, with his parents in their rugged homestead in a poor loghouse, and then he married from among his associates, a good girl, who afterwards did her best to help her husband on in the world. But somehow fortune always frowned, and the couple found life an uphill road.

At last, seemingly convinced that they could barely make a living on a farm, Mr. Cameron bestirred himself among his acquaintances and relatives and picked up enough money to purchase a passage for himself and his wife to Australia, which was then in a fever of excitement over the gold discovery. Nothing more was heard from the wanderers for five years, when all at once Mr. Cameron returned, and bearing with him a

A STRANGE BURDEN!

It comprised, first, a coffin with the embalmed remains of his dead wife, and second, unbounded sums of money, all in glittering gold!

His report was that instead of going to Australia as they had contemplated, they had finally brought up in the Fraser River region, at a point called Cariboo. That he there got possession of a claim, which he worked so successfully, and yielded so well, that he was the possessor of untold wealth, and he was in constant receipt of more. These facts were proven by the after events. Moreover, he said, with tears in his eyes, that his poor wife had died in that inhospitable country, and that his fortunate wealth and his love for her had prompted him to have her body embalmed that he might bring her home and bury her among friends. This was done; and then commenced a series of lavish expenditures on his part. First, he bought the old homestead and erected thereon, a grand and princely mansion, of Milwaukee brick, surrounded by the ample grounds with a unique and costly wall, purchased his parents and other relations comfortable homes, and seemed bent on the most lavish hospitality and generous use of his wealth in every direction. And still his store never seemed to diminish, and the people all blessed him, and copied him and united in calling him

CARIBOO CAMERON.

Everybody in the northern part of our state knows Cariboo Cameron, and he had not an enemy. But look at the sequel. After ten years of uninterrupted prosperity, during which he had risen to the very top of the social scale,

THERE CAME A CRASH!

And it came in an unthought of manner. One dreary night, late in the evening, a rap was heard on the door of

155

the Cameron mansion, and a poor weak woman was admitted, who begged for shelter for the night, and it was granted. Nothing special was thought of her, until next morning, as the family — the jovial husband, the happy wife whom he had married a year after his return, were seated at the breakfast table, the strange woman came into the room, walked straight in front of Cameron, and asked in an agonized tone,

"Do you know me?"

"My God, yes I do!" was the reply, and Cariboo Cameron fell senseless to the floor.

The woman was thrust hastily aside, and Cameron was restored to consciousness, but the moment he escaped from the house he left the country, and has not been heard of since then. That was last week.

And now comes a most horrible tale from this first sad wife, for the poor woman was none other than Cameron's wife, whom he had taken away so many years before. For the past ten years she has been the unwilling prisoner and wife of an Indian chief near Cariboo, to whom Cameron had

TRADED HER

for the claim that yielded him all his wealth.

That claim contained unbounded stores of gold, and its wealth was known to none but the Indian. After the bargain was struck Cameron supplied himself with great quantities of it, put the rest in the hands of a partner, who has worked it since, and sent Cameron's share to him.

THE COFFIN WAS TAKEN UP

and found to contain a mass of clay!

Of course the poor woman, who has been so foully dealt with, will step into the possession of the valuable property left on the St. Lawrence.

Who ever read a chapter more replete with incidents than this, and has all the additional interest of being fact.

It is hoped that the guilty fleeing wretch will be caught and dealt with as he deserves.[2]

Cameron reacted immediately. He sent instructions to the *Freeholder* to include an announcement in their next edition that on Tuesday, August 19, 1873, he would have the coffin of his wife exhumed and removed to Salem cemetery, mere yards down the road from Fairfield, where he would expose his dead wife's face to anyone who cared to witness it. In the meantime, he had stonemasons begin work immediately on a monument for Sophia that would be as recognizable as Fairfield.

Tuesday dawned hot and humid as only summer days along the St. Lawrence can. Several hundred onlookers had gathered at the cemetery for the spectacle. The outer wooden casket came apart easily and a tinsmith began cutting into the metal liner. Cameron was sweating. His very life depended on Sophia still being inside the coffin, that some greedy treasure hunter hadn't somehow opened it and removed her before sealing it up again. Red and white lines stood out on the back of his neck, and some thought he might be having a stroke. But when the tin was peeled back, there was Sophia's face, suspended just below the surface of the liquid, her eyes sunken but her face still showing traces of her youthful beauty. The heavy, silent air was rent by a shriek, "It's Sophie!" as Mrs. Groves recognized her dead daughter and swooned.

Relief flooded through Cameron like a spring freshet. It was as if the weight of the world had just been removed from his shoulders, and he felt scorn for all the petty people who had forced him into this bizarre situation, many of whom were filing past the coffin for a glimpse of the deceased. He ordered that the alcohol be poured off so that Sophia could return to that from which we all come.

"Dust to dust," he said.

And then they held her fourth and final funeral.

It was a fine memorial that Cameron ordered for the top of Sophia's sarcophagus. As this was to be her resting place for eternity, it was in the form of a symbolic bed, the head and foot connected by a vaulted slab and a single rail in the middle. It was cut from the whitest marble and took weeks to complete.

Sophia Cameron's grave in Summerstown. (PHOTO BY BILL GALLAHER)

Cameron considered it a work of art, yet it resulted in even more pettiness throughout the community. Some said that it was ostentatious, that if Sophia could see it from her special place in Heaven she would be embarrassed by it. Others complained that, considering what her husband had put her through, the poor woman deserved something far grander, a tomb perhaps.

Despite the relief Cameron felt, his life didn't improve much. The ordeal had left him heartsick, and he spiralled downward into a hell of his own creation that was one part guilt and another part contempt for almost everyone about him. He gave his money away even more freely. Those who had need of it came to Fairfield on the first of each month and if he felt they were honest, he would usually give them what they asked for. People still talked behind his back, but now they thought he belonged in the Provincial Lunatic Asylum in Toronto.

He made several investments that did not turn out very well, among them gold mines in the east, the Lachine Canal, and a sawmill that burned to the ground. They depleted his morale as much as they did his pocketbook, and he was compelled to take action before both were gone completely. He saw only one pathway to redemption and that was the long road leading back to Cariboo.

Actually, it wasn't so long any more. There was now a railroad that ran the breadth of the country and he could return there in style. Cameron and Christianne packed their belongings and in the spring of 1886, when he was 66 years old, they boarded the train bound for the west coast.

Victoria, when they arrived on May 10, had grown so much he scarcely recognized it. Gone were most of the muddy thoroughfares and the obsidian nights. Electric lamps lit

159

John Cameron in 1877 at 57 years of age. (COURTESY OF BC ARCHIVES A-01156)

macadamized streets plied by omnibuses, and there was talk that they would soon be replaced with streetcars. Debarking from the steamer at the old Hudson's Bay wharf he felt anonymous in the town where people had once known him by sight and everyone had called him "Cariboo" Cameron. But a newspaperman scanning the steamer's passenger list remembered his name, and the next day reported that "Old British Columbians experienced [an] agreeable surprise yesterday when the once familiar form of John A. Cameron appeared on the streets."

Then out of kindness or sycophancy added that he looked "as young as he did 23 years ago."[3]

It was a lie, of course. By no stretch of the imagination could Cameron's present manifestation be confused with the man he had been when he first came to Victoria. He was robust then, strong and sturdy, with a fine mane of brown hair, but the years had turned him soft and grey. He'd put on weight and there was a slight stoop to his shoulders. And it was certain that he didn't feel the way he had 23 years earlier. Nevertheless, he left Christianne to holiday in the capital while he went to the Big Bend country of the Columbia River. He staked a claim on Carnes Creek and worked it through a summer of driving rain with the passion, if not the strength, of his former self. But all he found was an old man growing even older.

His lung haemorrhaged, so he returned to Victoria early in November of '87. I met him there the following spring, not having seen him since that freezing February night nearly a quarter of a century before when we had argued till the small hours of the morning. Over hot whiskeys, he apologized for his obstreperousness and for having reneged on his promise to me. It was inexcusable, he said, adding that it was a very confusing time for him. Beyond that profound admission, he wouldn't elaborate.

I didn't expect him to. I couldn't begin to imagine what it must have been like to lose a wife and two children in such a short span of time — over any span of time — and feel responsible for it. It must have been a huge burden for him to carry. I wanted to tell him that, and let him know that regardless of his actions, I still held him in high regard. And I wanted to say that if I too hadn't been so obstinate on the day of Sophia's funeral, if I had signed the affidavit as he had asked me to, I might have saved him years of grief. But the words would not come from me.

I said only, "It's water under the bridge, John. You know I've always believed we should get on with our lives."

"Quite so," he agreed. "Quite so."

Later, Christianne said he had talked all winter of returning to Cariboo and reworking some of those old claims. He could hardly wait until he was feeling better and he could get under way. "Remember Twelve Foot Davis," he quipped feebly, mildly embarrassed about justifying his actions by using the exception to the rule.

"You're making a big mistake, John," I said. "It's a young man's game up there and you'll find nothing but a lot of frustration and heartache. Even Henry Davis would tell you that."

We were referring to Henry Fuller Davis who had noticed that two adjoining claims along Williams Creek were 12 feet longer than they were supposed to be — 212 feet instead of 200. He staked a claim on the extra 12 feet of ground and was rewarded with $15,000 in gold for his efforts. From that point on he was known as "Twelve Foot Davis." But it was an extremely rare occurrence, and hardly a good reason for what Cameron was about to do.

He wasn't seeking my advice, however. In fact, he wasn't interested in anyone's advice. He was determined to make one last grab for the golden ring and refused to see that it no longer hung in the same place. There was nothing more that I could say. It was typical of Cameron that once he'd made up his mind, there were few forces in the world able to change it. That July, he and Christianne set out for Barkerville.

It is difficult to know if Cameron felt discouraged upon their arrival, or the measure of it if he did. Cameronton had all but disappeared and what was left could not be distinguished from Barkerville. And like him, everything there was in a state of decline. They took rooms at the Barkerville Hotel.

I can only surmise that the next three months were a trial for Cameron, as he struggled with whatever it was that possessed him, and with trying to make an ailing, aged body do the strenuous physical labour that mining demanded. He was also disappointed to discover that the folks in Barkerville were every bit as good at gossiping as those back in Glengarry County. They'd just found something different to talk about, that's all. A rumour sped up and down the creek that he'd only come back because he was dead broke.

True to form, he said nothing to silence the disparaging whispers. One day in early November he returned to the hotel and complained to Christianne that he wasn't feeling "right." He was curiously light-headed and could see tiny dark shapes floating at the edge of his vision. She brought him some tea from a pot she'd made earlier, and turned the bedcovers back. After finishing the tepid drink he climbed into bed and was soon fast asleep. He never woke up again.

They buried him in the same hillside cemetery we'd started all those years before, when Peter Gibson died. Apparently, there was no shortage of mourners, but as one miner hastened to point out, more might have shown up had Cameron been rich.

Cameron's grave at Barkerville. (COURTESY OF BC ARCHIVES A-03776)

Chapter Eleven

A S I SAID earlier, after Cameron and I had argued about opening Sophia's coffin, I left to visit my family for a while. They were immensely pleased with my success in the goldfields, particularly my father who could not stop beaming the entire time I was home. Then, sometime in late February of 1864, I left for Cariboo. I was as compelled to return as a goose is to fly south in winter.

I spent the next 13 years there and saw Barkerville flourish as great fortunes were made and huge investments were lost. And I watched the town change.

I was there when the first Chinese arrived in '64, and once those first few got a foothold there was no stopping the rest of them. We considered them a strange lot, but then they thought we were, too. We could be so brazen and brash while they were reserved and polite. They thought us barbarians and called us "round-eyes" while we called them "slant-eyes" and "Chinks." Nevertheless, we got along reasonably well together by not mixing too much. Cameron had told me how abused they were in the California gold

*Barkerville in 1865. When Dutch Bill arrived on Williams Creek in 1861,
the forest covering the hills was thick and green.* (COURTESY OF BC ARCHIVES F-07013)

camps where many had met a violent end. On Williams
Creek, they were mostly ignored.

I was there when the Hurdy Gurdy Girls arrived during the
summer of '66. They were German dancing girls whose job it
was to lure miners into the saloons to spend their hard-earned
money on dancing and drinking. The girls charged a dollar a
dance, and received a percentage of whatever the miners spent
on liquor. They were not known for their subtlety when it came
to encouraging a customer to drink, and a man had to be careful when he entered a saloon where there were Hurdies. He
could easily go home drunk and penniless!

On a bright September afternoon in '68, I watched helpless-
ly as Barkerville burned to the ground. A stiff breeze pushed
the flames from building to building so fast that there wasn't a

thing any of us could do about it. In a matter of only a few hours, there wasn't much left of the town but a charred skeleton. The townsfolk were dumbfounded. They had believed that the buildings were constructed from a special kind of wood that was hard to burn. Fred Dally, the local photographer, said the fire was started when a miner knocked down a stovepipe as he tried to kiss a girl. (Dally kept that story to himself for fear the culprit would be lynched.) But if he hadn't started it, someone or something else would have. That summer had been hotter and drier than usual and people were so careless with fire that it was only a matter of time before it happened. As Dally had said, the town was doomed. Even so, the very next day it began rising out of the ashes and within a week 30 new buildings were up.

Twice, I was offered the job of Sheriff of Cariboo and turned it down. One of the responsibilities of that job was to make the arrangements for the execution of criminals sentenced to death, and that was employment I neither wanted nor needed.

I left Barkerville permanently in June of 1877, the year that I married my beloved Caroline. She had come west from Canada with her ailing brother and spent some time in California hoping that the drier weather would improve his failing health. They arrived in Victoria during the summer of '73, and she took a job as a teacher at the Methodist-run Sanford Chinese Mission School. I always wintered in Victoria and met her at a tea held by the Methodist Church. We were married on July 26, 1877.

I think I'm the only one still alive who was in Cariboo during its heyday so there's always someone asking me questions about it. They want to hear about the fabulous strikes of Billy

Barker, John Cameron, Ned Stout, or even Richard Willoughby, all the lucky ones, the winners in the great golden game.[1] They never ask about the unlucky ones, the men and women whose lives were destroyed. Few people, I suppose, want to hear about losers. But when I think of Cariboo, I also think of men like John Fraser.

John was the son of Simon Fraser whose last name was given to the river he explored. When his father died in 1862, young Fraser's family mortgaged their farm to send him to Cariboo in hopes of investing the money in some promising mine. He was a smart young man, an engineer, who at first set up shop in Cameronton. I suggested to him that the Prince of Wales mine was returning good dividends to its shareholders and if he also worked the dump box at ten dollars a day it might turn out quite well for him and his family. He did this, but was not content and spread his investments out into poorly producing mines.

When his payments on the farm fell behind, the bank foreclosed on the mortgage and his family was evicted. On the same day that he received the letter telling him that piece of bad news, he received another from his fiancée saying she had found a new love and was breaking off their engagement. John went mad. He paced the floor all night and in the morning slashed his wrists and jugular vein. As the blood poured from his body, he tried to run up the hill into the timber, but another miner and I caught him. We carried him to the doctor, who did his best to stitch the poor man up. It was too late. Twenty minutes later Fraser was dead. Twenty-four hours later, while he was being buried up by Peter Gibson, a claim that he had invested heavily in struck pay dirt.

There were others like John, men with great passion and a turn of bad luck who, even had they managed to hang on, would not have been any the richer for it. Yet their stories ought to be told too, along with Barker's and the rest, because they are also what Cariboo was about. It will never be known for sure exactly how many died by their own hand or for that matter, by a desperado's gun. Or how many were killed by the rugged canyon trails or some wild beast, by disease and starvation, or how many were just plain swallowed up by the unforgiving wilderness.

I can say with absolute certainty, though, that those who made fortunes were only a handful. Granted, more than a few might have made a decent living, but the creeks weren't very kind to most of the men who turned them upside down for gold. I don't know why it is that chance blesses the lives of some and not others. There are men, long since dead, who steered the same course I did, but never got anywhere except into an early grave. Why? There is more to it than hard work and brains, of that I am positive. I knew many men who worked every bit as hard as I did and were a great deal smarter, yet they had nothing to show for their trouble but aches and pains and disappointment. But I've always said that if a man can't handle the seemingly endless defeats, he'd be better off as a clerk, because the history of mining is a history of defeats punctuated by fleeting moments of outrageous victory. For miners, prosperity is a gypsy who sets up camp one night and is gone in the morning.

During the summer of 1907, in my 69th year, I returned to Barkerville for the first time in many years. The town was in the grip of a lingering death, but I went there solely to visit John Cameron's grave. With some effort, I climbed the hill to the cemetery, so full now, and so tamed since we cleared away the wilderness to bury Peter Gibson in '63. Cameron's grave, like many others, was surrounded by a white picket fence, the grass inside uncut and the marble headstone beginning to list. A light rain had started to fall as a dark bank of clouds moved in from the west. I stood there for a long time, unsure of why I'd really come. Perhaps because I had thought so many times that I would exhume my friend's coffin and take it home to Glengarry County, just as he had done for Sophia so many years before. It would be such an easy journey now, compared to that one. And yet maybe it wasn't that at all. Maybe it was only to prove to myself that Cameron's home, unlike Sophia's, was right there on that hillside among the mountains of Cariboo, overlooking the ground that had sated one great passion of his while it had stolen another.

Some say John died of a broken heart, but the truth is his body just gave out on him. Many of those same people also believe he died broke. That seems to be as much a part of his legend as his tremendous gold strike. For some strange reason, people want such stories to end that way. I can only presume it's because there is a better moral in it when they do. But that is not how John Cameron's story ends. It's true that he squandered the major part of his fortune, but since he worked hard for it, and gambled for it, I should think it was his to squander. It's also true that many of his investments turned sour, which required him to live in reduced circumstances, but he was a long way from being destitute. I know for a fact that he was to able leave Christianne in the financial circumstances to which she was accustomed.

There are also some who point to John's singular act of devotion as proof that people were somehow nobler of spirit in the olden days. I myself get caught in that trap from time to time. But there's no truth in it. People are people, as they have been down through the ages and as they always will be, full of greatness and pettiness, beauty and ugliness, innocence and guile. Only the conventions of time and place differ.

I suppose the question I am most often asked of Cameron is if he died a disappointed man. I believe the answer to that is yes. There isn't enough gold in the world to make up for the loss of a wife and two children. Moreover, men like Cameron are never satisfied. Even if, against all odds, he'd found a second pay streak, the satisfaction would have been short-lived because it was never really the gold he wanted in the first place. I believe there was a mystical side to Cameron that he neither understood nor explored, and which never progressed beyond dreams and silly superstitions. It was Big Chief Tonasket who told me, one night by the campfire on that long road to Lillooet, that a man always had to know where his centre was, and he tapped his chest over his heart so that his meaning was clear. Sometimes, he said, a man can get so distracted that he loses sight of it, and once it is lost, some men never find it again. Which is probably as good an explanation as any as to what happened to Cameron. The gold had distracted him, and turned him into the man he was and not the man he wanted to be. Then he lost sight of the path that led from one to the other. Caught up in such circumstances, how is it possible to be anything else but disappointed?

As for me, I'm always asked how much money I took from the creeks, and my answer is, I am in comfortable circumstances and always have been. I would never have had to work again after Cariboo had I wished not to, but I chose to continue in mining. It's all I have ever wanted to do since I first came west with my father and I have been involved in it ever since. After Barkerville, I went back to the Similkameen area and was the first to notice the huge coal deposits there. I bought a thousand acres at a dollar an acre, then staked out 27 squares miles of coal-bearing land, all of which is worth a pretty penny now. I also discovered some smaller coal deposits along Granite Creek, and I own a copper mine. I have several gold mines near the Similkameen River, one of which will yield nearly $20,000 to the ton if I can ever persuade the government to build a road to it. I bought a farm in Sardis on which to raise my family, but let me say straight up that I was never cut out to be a farmer. Nor was I meant to be a dandy or a gentleman. I'm a miner, pure and simple, and mining is my life. I came to that realization upon returning to Williams Creek after Sophia's burial, that for me it wasn't so much the taste of the bacon as it was the smell of it frying.

Throughout the years I've made the acquaintance of many interesting people, from down-and-out miners to prominent men and politicians of the highest office. I would not want to be thought boastful, but I can even count Sir James Douglas among my acquaintances. We first met back in Rock Creek, when he brought law and order to the Similkameen country. The miners there had refused to pay taxes, but he won them over with a promise to widen and extend the Dewdney Trail — which then joined Hope with Rock Creek — and a threat of returning with 500 marines if they didn't comply. I organized his meeting with the miners, and he displayed his gratitude by appointing me customs officer in Osoyoos.

But such things belong to the past. I am old now and sleep dogs my waking hours more often than I would care to admit. Caroline, my wife and companion for more than 40 years, died two years ago. She was a fine woman and my only regret is that my work took me away from her much too often. If there is such a place as Heaven, I know she was made welcome there.

The world has grown quieter around me. All our children have gone, grown up, with families and busy lives of their own. What once was an active farm is now but a few pleasant acres, and the old house that has known much joy engulfs me with silence. Eternity, ever the patient one, solemnly awaits my presence.

Robert Stevenson. (COURTESY OF BC ARCHIVES D-05306)

In 1898, how I envied those men who conquered the Chilkoot Pass on their way to the Klondike. Had I youthful legs, I would have been among them, for there is still a longing in my breast for such adventures. That they must go unfulfilled is the real tragedy of growing old, not death. Yet I find a modest compensation in writing this memoir, a vicarious thrill from what once was.

Curiously, as the gulf between the present and those early years broadens, the more vivid is my recollection of them. These days it is a rich and rewarding place in which to dwell, for the future is scant and the present rushes toward it with alarming speed. And though I can relive in my mind a dozen different stories, there is always one I return to more often than the rest: that of a good man, a preposterous promise, and its fulfilment.

Robert Stevenson
Sardis, BC
September 1922

Epilogue

Robert Stevenson died in November of 1922 at the age of 84. Of all the miners who mucked for Cariboo gold, he surely was one of the most successful, perhaps not so much in terms of the money he made, but in the life he led afterwards. He is buried in a family plot in a small cemetery near his home in Sardis, BC.

Endnotes

CHAPTER ONE

1. *British Colonist*, January, 16, 1862, p. 3.
2. Reksten, Terry, *More English than the English*, p. 65.
3. Quesnellemouth is an old name for the present city of Quesnel, situated where the Quesnel River joins the Fraser. The location was originally called "Quesnel," after a man who was with Simon Fraser during the descent of the river that now bears the explorer's name. It later became Quesnellemouth to distinguish it from Quesnelle Forks, located at the junction of the Quesnel and Cariboo rivers. Both places have now reverted to the original spelling.
4. Charles Morgan Blessing's gravesite can still be seen just off Highway 26, about halfway between Quesnel and Barkerville. Marked by a wooden headboard and enclosed by a white picket fence, it sits back in the forest, a solitary monument near a lonely stretch of road.

CHAPTER TWO

1. The Similkameen (River)-Boundary (Creek) country, includes the area from the Similkameen River, near present-day Princeton, east to Christina Lake.
2. The spelling differs depending on which side of the border one is on: the Canadian spelling is "Okanagan," while the Americans use "Okanogan."
3. There is a story connected to Diller that is the stuff of legends. Having used his mother's savings to finance his search for gold, he returned to his native Pennsylvania to find her farm being auctioned off to pay back taxes and the mortgage. Since he had not been home for many years, no one recognized him as he joined the bidding. His new-found wealth enabled him to outbid everyone, after which he greeted his tearful mother by returning the deed to her.

CHAPTER FIVE

1. *British Colonist*, April 18, 1862, p. 1.
2. F. W. Lindsay, *The Cariboo Story*, p. 21.
3. *Ibid.*, pp. 21-22.
4. Downs, Art, *Wagon Road North*, p. 66.
5. *Ibid.*
6. An alternative was to build a platform out of logs or lumber, but the work was the same.
7. According to records, the company set up on that date and known as the

"Cameron Claim" does not show Stevenson's name at all. It was not until three weeks later that the two names merge on the same claim and only for a while. A week after that, Stevenson transferred his shares to Sophia Cameron.

8. Just like William Dietz, and most of the other players on the Cariboo stage, this is but one version of Billy Barker's story with a hint of another. Stevenson was right in his suspicion, though, that there was more to Billy Barker than most people knew. The most recent and most thoroughly researched version says that Barker spent his early life as a riverman in Cambridgeshire, England, before migrating to North America and spending many years as a gold miner in California. He didn't find much gold but gained a wealth of experience and eventually moved north to the Fraser River in 1859. Cariboo was a natural progression from there.

CHAPTER SIX

1. "Scotch Jenny" or "Big Jenny," as she was also known, was buried in the Barkerville cemetery, her grave not far from John Cameron's. The spot where she fell to her death is marked for all to see on the walk between Barkerville and the Richfield courthouse.

CHAPTER SEVEN

1. Daniel O'Connell is one of the great figures of Irish history. Rising to prominence during the first half of the 19th century, he dedicated his life to Catholic emancipation. The record seems to indicate, though, that all three of O'Connell's daughters were married and living in Ireland during the period in question. That being said, if any of the three girls had had the potential to become Johanna Maguire, it would have been his youngest daughter, Betsy. As a child she was "extremely difficult — defiant, foul tempered, [and] hard hearted ..." and though she was married in 1831, ten years later there was talk of committing her to an asylum for "moral scrupulosity," the term in those days for religious mania. (Charles Trench, *The Great Dan*, pp. 129, 258) If somehow she did a complete turnabout from that religiosity and left her husband for British Columbia's gold country, there is no mention of it. She would have been around 50 years old at the time. On the other hand, O'Connell's reputation for siring illegitimate children, though never really proven, is as much a part of Irish folklore as is the leprechaun. It was said of him, "If the Queen was short soldiers for her army, all she had to do was apply to Dan to produce them," while a contemporary balladeer wrote, "He is now making children in Dublin by steam." (*Ibid.*, p. 281)

It is worthwhile to note here that according to Richard Thomas Wright (*Barkerville*, p. 42) there was a Barkerville prostitute named Johanna Maguire who was heading south that same winter and became lost for a week. She managed to relocate the trail but in the meantime lost the business earnings of $3,000 that she was packing out.

The question remains, though: was Johanna Maguire O'Connell's legitimate or illegitimate daughter? If so, what were her motives for coming to the colonies, and why did she assume a new identity? And why the identity of an ill-bred peasant rather than a member of the privileged class? What prevented her from revealing her background even under threat of punishment? Was she being paid to keep quiet? And if she wasn't one of O'Connell's offspring, then who was she? Someone with important connections, it would seem, since her request for a lawyer when she thought death was near is not one generally associated with the underclasses.

2. It was not uncommon to see animals abused, or worse, their corpses along the side of the road. Walter Cheadle, who travelled through this area in 1863, wrote in his diary that he had "spent the day looking at horses on the other side of the river. Some shockingly injured by bad packing & brutality; ribs broken, etc. They put one yearling filly's neck out today with the lasso when they threw it." (W.B. Cheadle, *Cheadle's Journal of a Trip Across Canada*, p. 226) On another day, he saw "6 horses lying dead in the road, hundreds probably a little way off in the bush," while the next day there were "12 dead horses and mules on the road." (*Ibid.*, p. 247)

CHAPTER EIGHT

1. A glaring inaccuracy, but not unusual for newspapers at the time.

CHAPTER NINE

1. Like its upstream counterpart, Richfield, Cameronton was short-lived. There was also a fourth town known as "Marysville" that sprang up below Cameronton, but other than the Richfield courthouse, there is nothing left to indicate that these places ever existed.

2. Though it was known then as the "Cameronton Cemetery," it is now generally referred to as the "Barkerville Cemetery." It is just a short walk from the present townsite. Now beautifully overgrown, the headstones tilt every which way and small white picket fences enclose many of the graves as well as each expansion of the cemetery. The marble marker erected later for Gibson stands there to this day and reads "Sacred to the Memory of Peter Gibson of Vankleek Hill County of Prescott Canada West who died July 24th, 1863 Aged 31 Years."

3. In today's money, Cameron's total haul would probably be worth in excess of $5,000,000.

4. Twelve years later, to the month, the *Pacific* would become BC's worst marine disaster when it sank after colliding with a sailing vessel near Cape Flattery. The exact number of people lost will never be known since ships in those days carried far more passengers than they were designed for. The passenger list said 287, but estimates have been as high as 500.

CHAPTER TEN

1. *Cornwall Freeholder*, 1865. Quoted in Pierre Berton, *The Wild Frontier*, p. 206.

2. *Sunday Times*, Syracuse, New York, 1873. Quoted in Pierre Berton, *The Wild Frontier*, pp. 208-9. Though outrageous by today's standards of reporting this story wasn't out of the ordinary for its time and would have been entirely believable. Newspapers regularly contained melodramatic, distorted, biased, even blatantly racist information. Add to that the fact that most people in the east would have thought BC to be as exotic a place as Mars, and there were all the ingredients of a story that might sell a lot of newspapers.

3. *British Colonist*, May 11, 1886, p. 3.

CHAPTER ELEVEN

1. Richard Willoughby was the discoverer of gold on Lowhee Creek, a small stream that drains into Jack of Clubs Lake, near Wells, BC. Born in Missouri, he led quite an adventurous life, being an Indian fighter at age 16 and a wagon train trail boss at 19. On his way into BC from Washington Territory, he is said to have fought a winning battle with Chief Tonasket and the Okanagans. He got as far north as Marble Canyon before rafting down the Fraser River (portaging around Hell's Gate) to the coast. From there he went to Cariboo and after striking pay dirt on Lowhee, he took it to a store owner who asked where he had found it.

He lied and said Williams Creek, but the store owner was familiar with gold from that area and insisted that it must have come from somewhere else, Willoughby refused to say where. Several miners overheard the exchange and followed him when he left. He knew he was being tailed and about midnight, he stopped to let the others catch up to him. "Is everybody here?" he asked, and when someone muttered that there were still stragglers back on the trail, Willoughby said he'd wait for them. When everyone had arrived, he announced, "This is it boys. This is my claim I'm standing on, and you can stake on either side of me!"

Bibliography

Abernathy Mellows, Carol. "The Clash of Cultures; 1800 to 1858," in Webber, Jean, ed. *Okanagan Sources*. Theytus Books Ltd., Penticton, BC, 1990.

Basque, Garnet. *Ghost Towns and Mining Camps of the Boundary Country*. Sunfire Publications, Langley, BC, 1992.

———. *Gold Panner's Manual*. Heritage House Publishing Company, Surrey, BC, 1996.

Berton, Pierre. *The Wild Frontier, More Tales From The Remarkable Past*. Penguin Books, Canada, 1978.

Cheadle, Walter B. *Cheadle's Journal of a Trip Across Canada 1862 - 1863*. M.G. Hurtig Ltd., Edmonton, AB, 1971.

Downs, Art. *Wagon Road North*. Heritage House Publishing Company Ltd., Surrey, BC, 1993.

Ellis, John J. *The Fernwood Files*. Orca Book Publishers, Victoria, BC, 1989.

Gregson, Harry. *A History of Victoria 1842 - 1970*. The Victoria Observer Publishing Company, Victoria, BC, 1970.

Higgins, David William. *The Mystic Spring and other Tales of Western Life*. William Briggs, Toronto, ON, 1904.

Johnson, R. Byron. *Very Far West Indeed*. Sampson, Low, Marston, Low, & Searle, London, 1872. (Reprinted 1985.)

Kilian, Crawford. *Go Do Some Great Thing, The Black Pioneers of British Columbia*. Douglas & McIntyre, Vancouver, BC, 1978.

Lindsay, F.W. *The Cariboo Story*. The Quesnel Advertiser, Quesnel, BC, 1958.

McKelvie, B.A. *Tales of Conflict*. Heritage House Publishing Company, Surrey, BC, 1985.

Marks, Paula Mitchell. *Precious Dust: The Saga of the Western Gold Rushes*. William Morrow, New York, 1994.

Patenaude, Branwen C. *Trails to Gold*. Horsdal & Schubart, Victoria, BC, 1995.

Patterson, T.W. *Outlaws of Western Canada*. Mr. Paperback, Langley, BC, 1982.

Pethick, Derek. *British Columbia Disasters*. Mr. Paperback, Langley, BC, 1982.

———. *Victoria: The Fort*. Mitchell Press Limited, Vancouver, BC, 1968.

Reksten, Terry. *More English than the English*. Orca Book Publishers, Victoria, BC, 1986.

Rothenburger, Mel. *The Wild Mcleans*. Orca Book Publishers, Victoria, BC, 1993.

Skelton, Robin. *They Call it the Cariboo*. Sono Nis Press, Victoria, BC, 1980.

Sterne, Netta. *Fraser Gold 1858!* Washington State University Press, Pullman, WA, USA, 1998.

Stevenson, Robert. "A Pioneer of '59," in Walkem, W. Wymond. *Stories of Early British Columbia*. News Advertiser, Vancouver, BC, 1914.

Trench, Charles Chenevix. *The Great Dan*. Jonathan Cape, London, 1983.

Wade, Mark S. *The Cariboo Road*. The Haunted Bookshop for Hugh F. Wade, Victoria, BC, 1979.

Wright, Richard Thomas. *Barkerville Williams Creek, Cariboo*. Winter Quarters Press, Duncan, BC, 1993.

NEWSPAPERS

British Colonist, Victoria, BC.